MAIDEN VOYAGE

SARAH JANE

MAIDEN VOYAGE

A *Titanic* Story

Scholastic Inc.

ISBN 978-1-338-22665-2

10 9 8 7 6 5 4 3 2 1   18 19 20 21 22

Printed in the U.S.A.   40
First printing 2018

The text type was set in 11/20 Sabon MT Std
Book design by Nina Goffi

For the brave souls aboard the
Titanic's maiden voyage

1

ISABELLA JAMES

3:00 a.m. Wednesday, April 10, 1912

"Hurry now," Isabella James's mother rushed her out the door and into the cold, damp predawn air. "We can't be late." She hoisted a full carpetbag onto her arm.

Late for what? Isabella wondered. The tightness in her mother's voice kept her from asking the question aloud. She stumbled into the London streets and blinked, letting her eyes adjust to the dark. There were no streetlights in their neighborhood, and her thin coat did little to ward off the biting spring cold. She longed to crawl right back into her bed, the only warm place in the tiny apartment she shared with her parents, but the door was already closed and she could hear her father turning the key.

Isabella's mother clutched her hand as they began to move in a small herd through the streets of East London. It was clear that they had a destination, that her mother was leading them somewhere.

Isabella fleetingly wondered if her parents had found her a job. Things had been hard lately. The coal strike seemed unending, and her father hadn't worked in weeks. And worse, Isabella was concerned he would not be healthy enough to return to the mines when the strike ended. She heard her father cough, as if agreeing with her thoughts.

Of course Isabella would have been more than happy to work, to do whatever she could to put food on the table and a fire in the stove. Already she was assisting her mother taking in laundry and sewing, though she knew it was not enough. She honestly hoped her family had found her a job. But what sort of job required leaving home in the middle of the night?

And what sort of job required a packed carpetbag?

Isabella hurried to keep up with her mother's rapid pace. She turned back to her father, who was lagging and breathing heavily. "Are you all right, Papa?" she asked quietly.

Francis James nodded, punctuating the gesture with another ragged cough. Worry seeped into Isabella like the damp cold. Her chest was tight, her mouth full of unspoken words.

"Mother, we're moving too quickly," she said softly. Her mother slowed for an instant, but only an instant.

"We have no choice," she answered, her voice a high-pitched squeak. "We mustn't miss the train."

The train?

Isabella squinted, trying to see her mother's face, to read something in her eyes. Though the black sky was turning gray with the promise of dawn, it was still dark. She could not make out her expression, but saw her raise a hand to her cheek, to wipe at something shiny. Isabella sucked in her breath. She had never seen her mother cry.

2

LUCY MILES

11:30 a.m. Wednesday, April 10, 1912

"The ship's been fitted out with every luxury imaginable and they say she's absolutely unsinkable!"

Lucy Miles overheard the excitement of the passengers around her as they crossed the elevated gangplank and moved toward the first-class entrance of the White Star Line's glorious *Titanic*. Not only was she the largest ship ever built, she was the grandest. And she was brand-new!

Lucy linked her arm through her mother's. "Did you hear that, Mama?" she asked in a cheerful voice. "That gentleman said the *Titanic* is unsinkable!" Lucy hoped the words would comfort her mother. "Isn't that right, Father?" She looked over her shoulder at her father with a broad smile, hoping he would offer some reassurance of his own. Her mother was easily overwhelmed—especially lately—and what with the noise, the train ride to Southampton, the crowds swirling below them, and the seven-day sea crossing ahead, Elisabeth Miles already looked rather pale.

"Father?" Lucy repeated a bit louder. But Phillip Miles didn't seem to hear her. He was staring intently into the crowd of people below who had come to see the massive ship off on its maiden voyage, as though looking for something. Or someone. Lucy's smile faded as she studied his face. His moustache was so large it hid most of his mouth, but it was not big enough to cover his twisted scowl.

Never mind, Lucy told herself, turning back to her mother and the massive *Titanic*. Her father just needed to get away from London, to leave his business concerns behind. Once he sailed away from the day-to-day distractions, the three of them would be able to have the family holiday she had longed and waited for. After all, they were traveling to America! To New York City, where her mother had been born. Lucy was looking forward to staying with her uncle Julian and aunt Millie, and all of her cousins.

Lucy felt her mother teeter a bit on the gangplank, and deftly steadied her. "What is it?" she asked, following her mother's backward gaze. Elisabeth did not answer, but it was clear that her husband's scowl had caused the misstep. Lucy opened her mouth to speak, trying to think of something to distract her mother from her father's pronounced sourness, when Abby O'Rourke, their new maid, spoke first.

"Oh, look, Lady Elisabeth!" the maid cried, her blue eyes wide. She shifted one of the hatboxes she was carrying—they were too delicate to leave to the stewards—so she could point to a gray-striped cat making her way down another, far less busy gangplank below them with a kitten in her mouth. The small mama cat made the trip three times as the Miles party made their way slowly up the other gangplank, settling each of her babies in an empty cargo crate on the dock.

"She's a diligent mother, isn't she?" Elisabeth noted.

"Indeed," Abby replied. "Although I wonder why she's disembarking with her little family before we've even set sail?"

"Perhaps the *Titanic* is so new there aren't enough mice on board to keep the kittens fed," Lucy offered, turning back to her mother. But Elisabeth wasn't looking at the cats any longer. She was gazing intently into the crowd of people below.

"Phillip, that man there. He's calling your name," she said, pointing at someone in the crowd.

Indeed, the man in the crowd was hard to miss. He was large and rough-looking, with a broad face. He waved his arms angrily and shouted, "Miles! Phillip Miles!"

Lucy turned to her father to ask who the man was, but he didn't acknowledge her. He focused his attention in the precise opposite direction, and appeared suddenly eager to get to the top of the gangplank and through the carved double doors.

Looking back, Lucy caught sight of the man once more and saw him take off his cap and wave it in the air, signaling someone else while still pointing at her father. She tried to look in the direction the man was waving and thought she saw a second red-faced man lifting his chin to signal back, but her view was cut off when her father stepped in front of her and entered the *Titanic*.

"My, my, what a ship!" he exclaimed, his scowl turning into a stiff smile. "White Star clearly spared no expense on this enormous tub!"

Lucy thought *tub* was an odd word for such a glorious liner, but she had to agree with her father's assessment as she joined him inside the lovely white-paneled room. The carved ceilings, the plush carpet, the turned bannisters . . . everything was opulent down to the tiniest details! The *Titanic* was so ornate she felt as if she'd boarded a floating palace, and all thoughts of the shouting man promptly disappeared.

3

ABIGAIL O'ROURKE

11:45 a.m. Wednesday, April 10, 1912

Abby O'Rourke craned her neck as she made her way toward the *Titanic*'s first-class entrance. But she wasn't trying to get a look inside the beautiful ship—she was searching for the large yellow steamer trunk that was supposedly being loaded with the rest of the Miles family luggage. She'd checked the tag herself, making sure it had the red-and-white circular label with the correct stateroom. But hadn't Master Miles complained that luggage on steamships often went missing? With over thirteen hundred passengers and their many trunks, suitcases, crates, and even medicine chests, it was a wonder that anything made it to its proper place.

Apprehension prickled at the back of Abby's neck. The yellow steamer could *not* get lost.

"Abigail, is everything all right?" Miss Lucy was peering at her intently, which unnerved Abby even further. She still hadn't grown accustomed to working for a girl the same age she was, but she was trying to adjust . . . to so many things.

"Of course, Miss," she replied. "It's just so beautiful." Abby was embarrassed that she'd let her distraction show. Her mother—the Mileses' previous maid—would have never let her own thoughts get in the way of her work. "*My concerns are of no concern*," Maggie had explained to her daughter more than once. Abby knew the same was supposed to be true of her. She was in service now. Her opinion had no place, and her attention was to be on Mistress Elisabeth and Miss Lucy, and nothing else, at all times.

Abby closed her eyes for the briefest of moments, pushing back the grief that lived just below the surface. If her mother were still alive, Abby wouldn't even *be* a maid.

Inside the first-class entrance, a smartly dressed steward was handing the gentlemen flowers to wear in their lapels. He extended a perfect yellow carnation to her master, but Phillip Miles batted it away. "I don't wear flowers," he gruffed.

The steward looked momentarily taken aback, but quickly adjusted his face into an unreadable expression. "Of course, sir. It's entirely up to you."

"I should say so," Master Miles replied. Abby bristled at her master's rudeness. Though it was hardly unexpected, it was completely unnecessary. The man was only doing his job!

Phillip Miles stepped up to a second steward and handed over three first-class boarding cards and one second-class boarding card with a flourish. "Stateroom for us," he said. "Nothing but the best for my girls. And the maid will be fine on a separate deck. Isn't that right, O'Rourke?"

"Of course, sir," Abby replied.

"We are offering tours of the first-class sections of the ship if you'd like to accompany your steward," the man holding the boarding passes said, gesturing toward a line of young men in uniform.

"Oh, that sounds wonderful!" Lucy exclaimed. "May we, Father?"

"I could start to unpack your things," Abby said, seizing the opportunity. A little time away from the Miles family was precisely what she needed.

"You can do more than just start," Master Miles replied

brusquely. "You can bloody well finish!" Abby stood up straighter. She was careful not to react to her master's swearing, but saw the ladies around them cringe. "You'd think a girl your age would be quick, and yet you're so much slower than your mother ever was."

"I don't know about a tour," Mistress Elisabeth said, interrupting her husband's rant. "I'm exhausted from all the commotion."

Lucy took ahold of her mother's hand. "Oh, Mother, please?" she pleaded. "I'm sure we'd only be in Abigail's way, and there's so much to see."

Abby much preferred Miss Lucy calling her by her first name. In her mind, *O'Rourke* would always be her mother's service name, not her own.

Elisabeth smiled wanly at her only child. "Oh, all right, Lucy," she said with a little nod. "But only if it's not terribly long."

"You can slip out of the tour whenever you like," the steward assured them. "The time spent is at your discretion, of course."

Abby tried not to show her relief at the realization that she really was going to get a reprieve from the entire Miles family, if only for a few minutes.

"Well, what are you waiting for, girl?" Master Miles barked at Abby as he prodded his wife and daughter toward the steward who was to take them on their personalized tour. "This voyage is not a vacation for you. I expect you to be as industrious on the *Titanic* as you are in London. Get to work!"

Abby narrowed her eyes at her master's back as he and his family walked away. He never missed an opportunity to shout at her, or point out her failings. Or anyone else's, for that matter.

As the group passed through the far set of double doors she heard passengers remarking on the glass-domed staircase. Everyone, it seemed, was enthralled by the Grand Staircase. Abby wanted to pause and gaze at the beautiful sight herself—it was a wonder with its intricately carved oak, sweeping curves, and winged figure lamp—but she had more pressing matters to deal with.

After getting directions from another steward, she hurried to board an elevator behind the opulent staircase. She suspected the elegant lift was the fastest route to the Mileses' suite, and she did not know how long her freedom would last. Though she'd only been doing her mother's job for a couple of months, Abby understood that Elisabeth Miles was prone to fits of fatigue and might remain on the tour for only a few minutes before retiring to her stateroom to rest.

Following the steward's instructions, she found the Mileses' stateroom on B deck. The small plaque on the door said "Gregorian," and when Abby stepped inside she couldn't help but gasp. The suite was glorious! It had curved paneled walls covered in golden damask with carved arches outlined in gold, and the paint on the shining white trim was so fresh she could still smell it. The fittings were more ornate and beautiful than those inside the Mileses' mansion in London! The family would have plenty of space during their voyage, for their quarters included two dressing rooms, two bedrooms, a sitting room, and a private bathroom.

Before Abby could latch the door there was a rap, and two harried-looking bellboys, not much older than she was, appeared to deliver the family's luggage. Abby bit her lip as she scanned the pile of suitcases and trunks, looking for something yellow . . .

Finally, she spotted it. "This one here belongs in cabin D twenty-two," she told the bellboy, looking at her boarding pass to confirm. The boy looked from the steamer, to her, and back to the steamer. He double-checked the label.

"You sure?" he asked doubtfully. "The label says it belongs right here."

Abby couldn't tell if the bellboy was lazy or worried about getting into trouble, but she straightened up, squared her shoulders, and tried to speak with authority. "D twenty-two," she repeated, rapping three times on the trunk for emphasis.

"Oh, all right," the bellboy agreed, shrugging. He took a breath and hoisted the trunk. "What do you have in here, rocks?" he asked as he steadied his legs against the weight.

Abby felt a tingle of alarm, but did not pause in situating the Mileses' luggage for orderly unpacking. There were so many cases! She opened the trunks with the gowns and overcoats and hurriedly hung them in the large armoire. With that accomplished, she moved on to neatly placing undergarments, hats, and gloves in the many drawers. She unpacked pair after pair of shoes, running a cloth over them as she did. She worked quickly, unpacking books and files and hairbrushes and hand mirrors. There were so many things to arrange it felt like she would never get to her own unpacking. Lastly, she set up Mistress Miles's medicine chest, organizing her most recent tonics.

The moment the last case was emptied and put away, Abby hurried out of the stateroom in search of her own cabin and the yellow steamer. She rushed down a corridor, a set of stairs, and another corridor. But wait—how did she get all the way down to E deck? Turning back, she went up a flight of stairs and found D deck. But here the cabin numbers were too high.

Her worry mounting, Abby backtracked again and somehow found the correct corridor. And then, finally, D 22. Letting out an enormous sigh of relief, she pushed open the door.

4

ISABELLA

11:50 a.m. Wednesday, April 10, 1912

Isabella stood in the mass of swirling strangers on gangway E with tears streaming down her pale face.

"You're late," the scowling doctor barked. He peered into her eyes and ears, jerking her head back and forth as he checked her for signs of illness. "I don't know why you people think you can arrive at the last minute and expect to pass your medical exam in time to board. We can't have infectious diseases ruining *Titanic*'s maiden voyage."

The Titanic, Isabella thought, fighting back a fresh wash of tears that blurred the enormous boat looming before her.

"You won't be allowed on if we find anything, you

know," the doctor snapped as his rough hands began to search her dark curls for lice.

I don't want to board! Isabella shouted in her head. *I want to go home!*

The doctor leaned forward, peering through a magnifying glass at her scalp. His foul breath lingered in front of her face, nearly making her gag. Squeezing her eyes shut and trying not to inhale, she silently prayed that he would find lice and she would be turned away.

It hadn't been until they'd reached the docks at Southampton and the massive ship loomed into view that Isabella had begun to grasp her parents' intentions. And even then it had been too horrible for her to believe. She was being shipped off to the other side of the Atlantic! She'd turned to them as it dawned on her, searching their faces for a sign that it wasn't true. That she wasn't such a burden to them that they would have to send her away . . .

"But, Mama!" She hadn't been able to say more than that.

Ruth James held up a hand to silence her child. "It has been decided, and it is for the best," she'd said. Her voice quavered as she shoved a third-class ticket and an envelope into Isabella's hand. "It's a seven-day journey to New York," she'd said. "You are to open this envelope the day before you arrive in America, and not a moment before. Do you understand?"

It was then that Isabella had started to cry. She'd nodded her understanding when words failed her.

"Do you promise?" her mother had asked again.

"I promise, Mama," she'd finally managed to croak raggedly.

With that, her mother had pulled her into a tight hug. "We love you more than anything in this world," she'd whispered, kissing her hair. "Never forget that."

Her father had brushed away tears with a shaking hand and pulled her to his chest. "Keep your head up, love," he'd said. "And know that America will be lucky to have you."

"I said you've been cleared," the doctor said loudly, pulling Isabella out of her memory. He gave her a shove up the gangplank and she stumbled away from the lingering stench of his breath. "Now board."

Isabella held tightly to her ticket, the envelope, and her carpetbag as she moved up the gangplank in a throng of what appeared to be mostly Swedish and Irish families. She wiped her damp cheeks with the back of her hand and turned to look back at her parents one last time. They were leaning into each other so closely they appeared to be a single form. Her father coughed into his handkerchief, folding it carefully in a useless attempt to hide the blood. There was no disguising the severity of his illness—the small scrap of fabric had been coughed into so many times it was stained through. Ruth James stood stock-still next to her husband, shedding silent tears. It was clear from their faces that they didn't want her to go. And yet . . .

Isabella felt a tightening in her chest. If her parents sent her away, how could she be sure she would ever see her father again? Who would help her mother care for him? Who would be there for her mother if he passed?

Beside her on the gangplank, a small boy clutched his mother's hand. Behind her, a family spoke excitedly in a language she did not recognize. Caught in the crowd, Isabella had never felt so alone. She had never felt so heavyhearted. What would become of her, all by herself on the biggest ship ever built, without a single acquaintance?

Blinking back more tears, Isabella boarded the F deck of the *Titanic* in a mob, turning back just in time to see the massive gangplank she'd walked up being pulled away from the side of the ship. There would be no going back.

Her fate was sealed.

5

ABBY

11:55 a.m. Wednesday, April 10, 1912

"Hullo!" a young woman called to Abby the moment she entered the cabin. Abby was so surprised she nearly stepped back into the hall and closed the door. She'd assumed, foolishly she now realized, that she would have her own berth. What in the Lord's good name had made her think that miserly Master Miles would pay for a servant to have a private room? She steadied herself and quickly scanned the compartment, her eyes coming to rest on the yellow steamer. It had been safely delivered as promised.

"Cat got your tongue, has it?" her new roommate asked cheerfully. She was wearing sensible traveling clothes and had brown wavy hair that looked like it had been tucked into a tidy bun at one point, but was now struggling to break free . . . and succeeding. "Well, I'm glad you're finally here! Can you believe how large this cabin is? I think we could easily fit a third berthmate!"

In addition to the ample size, the furnishings were fine. Abby blinked at the mahogany bunk bed, floral curtains, and porcelain sink with running water.

She coughed into her hand, grateful that her new acquaintance didn't give her a moment to respond.

"Well, welcome aboard! I'm Constance Gruenfeld, housemaid to the Litchfeld family. Though there's not much for me to clean while I'm on board. It appears the *Titanic* has servants for everything . . . 'cept dressing. Only the lady's maids and valets and nurses have to work, the poor things. Thank goodness I'm not . . ." She paused briefly, eyeing Abby's black-and-white uniform.

"Oh, sorry. Looks like this won't be a holiday for you like it will be for me!" she barreled on. "I won't have to work until we reach the other shore! This is my first crossing. How about you? Have you ever been aboard a ship like this?" Constance gestured broadly around the room.

"No, I—"

"What am I saying?" Constance answered her own question. "Of course you haven't been on a ship like this! There's never *been* a ship like this! She's a one of a kind, she is."

Abby agreed. The *Titanic* was a marvel! But it was rather difficult to get a word in edgewise . . . even just to say *yes*.

"Is that your trunk? It's awfully large for a maid, isn't it?" Constance babbled, raising her chin at the yellow steamer that had been left not far from the door. "Though I suppose it fits right in here, really. Everything on the *Titanic* is enormous!" She dropped her hands to her sides, suddenly looking a bit tired, perhaps from all her talking. But a moment later she started up again. "I'd wager these accommodations are as fine as any in first class on another ship . . ."

Abby steadied herself against the partition between the small built-in couch and the door. She inched closer to the yellow trunk and discreetly made sure the tiny holes running along one side were out of her berthmate's view.

"So, are you going to introduce yourself?" Constance asked.

Abby let out a small laugh and stepped forward. "Yes." She held out a hand. "I'm Abigail O'Rourke. Please forgive my manners—I'm afraid I'm a bit overwhelmed! I got quite lost on my way here after having to unpack for—"

"I know what you mean!" Constance interrupted while setting out her toilet kit. "I don't know how I will ever find my way about!"

"You might be able to join one of the tours on B deck," Abby blurted, seeing a way to solve two problems at once.

"Tours?" Constance echoed.

Abby nodded. "There was one about to start when I left," she said, and added on a whim, "led by a handsome steward no less." It was a bit cheeky, but it did the trick.

Constance set her hairbrush down on the vanity, her curiosity piqued. "Handsome, you say?" she mused. A sly smile spread across her face, lighting up her hazel eyes. "I suppose there will be time to settle in later, won't there? Would you like to come along?"

Abby shook her head, feigning disappointment. "I'm afraid I have just a few minutes to unpack myself before I have to get back to my mistress." *It's not a lie*, she thought.

"And you have plenty to unpack!" Constance moved toward the yellow steamer to give it a thump, but Abby stepped protectively between the chatty girl and the trunk.

"Sorry," she apologized for her strange behavior. "I'm

just rather sentimental. This trunk belonged to my dear departed mother." *Also not a lie*, she told herself.

Constance reached out a hand to touch Abby's shoulder. "Oh, Love, I'm so sorry," she said kindly. Then, in an instant, her eyes brightened again. "Well, I'd better be off if I'm to catch the handsome tour guide!" she chirped, giving Abby a wink.

As soon as Constance was gone, Abby latched the cabin door and unlatched her yellow steamer, giving it four sharp knocks. In an instant, the lid flew open and a very small, very red-faced boy emerged.

"Finally!" he hooted. "I've been in here for days!"

Abby laughed and threw her arms around her younger brother in relief. It had only been hours—but to Felix, locked up in a steamer, it must have felt like days. Honestly, it had been an excruciatingly long period of time for her, too. But now he was on board, and he was all right! "It's a good thing you're small for your age," she mused happily.

Felix shook his head, rejecting this idea. His gray eyes were serious. "I'm not small, I'm seven."

Abby laughed. "Fine. It's a good thing you're seven and can fit in a trunk."

"A very large trunk," Felix corrected. "That girl said so."

"Could you hear everything?" Abby asked.

"Yes!" he cried excitedly, jumping out of the trunk and exploring the cabin. "Blimey, this room is fit for a king!" he cried as he opened the drawers next to the washbasin and turned on the faucets. "Cold and hot!" He switched them off and raced to the door. "Everyone is talking about how big the *Titanic* is," he reported. "And how grand. I want to go on a tour, too!" He twisted the handle, but the door remained locked.

Abby felt a wave of panic. She'd been so preoccupied with getting Felix on board undetected that she hadn't considered how difficult it would be to keep him secreted away for a whole week. And with a roommate!

"Just how big is the *Titanic*?" Felix persisted.

"Enormous," Abby replied. "But I'm afraid *you* won't be seeing much more than these four walls."

Felix scowled and hopped up onto the couch. He turned his large gray eyes on his sister, looking utterly innocent.

"Don't give me that look, Felix," Abby said firmly, though even as she spoke the words she wondered how she'd gone from playful sibling to responsible adult in the blink of an eye.

That's what happens when your parents die. The

thought came so quickly it startled her with its brutal honesty. She pushed it away just as fast.

"We can't risk anyone finding out you're on board. Not after all the trouble we went through to get you here. You did a good job keeping quiet and hidden in that trunk—and now you're going to have to do the same in this cabin," she explained. "That means no going out. That means not a peep when anyone else is about. Not even Constance, our new roommate, can know you're here."

While she spoke, doubt began to swell in the pit of Abby's stomach. Felix couldn't sit still for five minutes. How was she going to contain him for seven whole days? And yet, what choice did they have?

When Master Miles had first asked Abby to accompany the family to America on the *Titanic*, she had been thrilled. She'd long dreamed of a new life across the Atlantic—there were opportunities for a girl in America! But her excitement had vanished when she'd remembered her brother, whom she loved dearly and, without their parents, was solely in her care.

James O'Rourke, their seaman father, had left on a cargo voyage just over a year ago and never returned. When they'd gotten the notice that he had died in a shipwreck, her mother, Maggie O'Rourke, had been devastated. They all had. But none of them could have known that Maggie herself would be gone less than a year later, leaving Abby and Felix alone in the world. They didn't know how she died. There was no long illness, and no money for a service. There was just their tiny apartment in London, and a job in the Miles household for Abby if she wanted it.

Abby had no desire to be a lady's maid, or work for the Miles family. But again, what choice did she have?

None. Nor did she have a choice about smuggling her little brother on board the *Titanic*. When she'd asked Master Miles if Felix might accompany them to America, he had laughed cruelly. "You expect me to pay for his passage?"

"But where will he stay while I'm gone?" she'd asked pleadingly.

"A workhouse, of course."

Abby knew perfectly well what the workhouses were like for young boys—the poor children spent their days breaking stone, or crushing bones. They passed nights crowded into dorms, sharing diseases. She'd heard that sometimes the boys were so hungry they'd fight over the marrow left in the bones they were meant to grind. After everything they'd been through, Abby couldn't let that happen to her brother. She'd briefly considered going to Mistress Miles to ask if she could persuade her husband, but her mistress was weak and not likely to stand up to her husband, and if Master Miles found out she had gone behind his back, she would have been sacked for sure, and then what would they have done?

As if Master Miles discovering that I've stowed Felix aboard won't yield the same result! she thought.

He won't find out, she told herself. *He can't. We will make it to America.* Felix just had to stay hidden for a single week so she could properly attend to the Miles women—a challenging task at best. It would not be easy, but it had to be done.

"You need to climb up here and take a rest," Abby said to Felix, who was pouting on the bench. She patted the upper bunk.

"What do you think I've been doing in that bloody trunk all day?" he replied, annoyed.

"Watch your language, Felix," Abby scolded.

"Sorry," Felix replied. "But it was bloody awful." He raised his eyebrows, realizing he'd said it again, and slapped a hand over his mouth. "Sorry," he repeated, though it was muffled by his hand.

Abby leaned in and gave him a kiss on the forehead. "Please just stay here and stay quiet," she instructed. "If you're found out, they'll throw us both overboard."

Felix's eyes went round. "Really?"

Abby nodded. "Really." She slid the curtain closed and unlatched the cabin door. "Just stay put," she said firmly as she pulled the door shut and stepped back into the corridor, nearly bumping into a young steward passing behind her.

"Don't worry, miss," the steward said with a wink. "The cabins on the *Titanic* aren't in the habit of wandering off."

Abby felt her cheeks flame, though whether it was because of her stowaway secret or the steward's warm brown eyes and crooked smile she could not be sure. She nodded quickly and hurried away, praying that the young man hadn't heard her little brother's voice.

LUCY

4:00 p.m. Wednesday, April 10, 1912

"Doesn't it all sound delicious?" Lucy looked over the food choices in the Café Parisien. *Roast squab and cress. Chilled asparagus vinaigrette. Salmon mousseline.* Her mouth watered and her eyes lingered on the chocolate éclairs listed near the bottom.

"Look, Mother!" she pointed at the treat.

Seated across from her, Elisabeth Miles looked less enthusiastic. "I'm afraid I don't have much of an appetite," she said with a weak smile. Lucy gave a slight nod of understanding and set down her own menu. She gazed out the windows. The café, which was adjacent to the à la carte restaurant, offered a magnificent view of the water through open windows along the length of one side. Trellises wound with ivy adorned the walls on the opposite side of the long room, which was furnished with white rattan tables and chairs and peppered with palms, creating the effect of a covered veranda.

"My stomach is still in fits after that accident," Elisabeth complained, oblivious to the charming atmosphere.

"Near accident," Lucy corrected gently. She stole a look at her father, who was holding his menu in front of his face like a wall, clearly not paying attention to the conversation. "We should feel comforted that our captain was skilled enough to steer us out of danger."

She smiled at her mother as if she hadn't a fear in the world, though in truth the near collision with the *New York* had been more than a little unnerving. They had only just left the dock and were maneuvering out of the harbor, which was unusually crowded with moored boats due to the coal strike, when the *New York* was pulled into the great ship's wake. The suction force of the *Titanic* was so powerful it snapped six of *New York's* hawsers and pulled it within two feet of the huge liner before it was edged away by a tug at the last possible second. Lucy and her mother had watched the whole thing from the deck, and Lucy felt her shoulders clench at the memory of the near accident.

"And what would have happened if we'd collided?" her mother asked.

"Stop fussing, Elisabeth," Phillip snapped, apparently listening after all. "You heard Ismay say it would take more than a gash in the flank of his prize beast to even slow her down."

It was true—J. Bruce Ismay, manager of the White Star Line and overseer of the *Titanic*'s construction—was not only on the maiden voyage of the ship but also on deck during the close call. He'd comforted the passengers with his confident assurances about the ship.

"And who would know better than Ismay?" Phillip asked, setting down his menu and raising a hand to summon the waiter. Before Lucy could even offer a word about what she wanted, he had ordered for all three of them. There would be no éclairs, apparently.

Lucy let out a tiny sigh. He'd selected consommé for her mother, which might settle her stomach, but he was so surly she didn't dare request what she wanted. At least everything on the menu was appealing! Additionally, it struck her as a terrible waste to be grumpy on such a beautiful day . . . on such a grand ship . . . on the eve of adventure!

It hasn't even been a day yet, Lucy reminded herself. *It might take him a while to unwind.* She tried to think back to a time when she'd known a more relaxed and smiling version of her father, but found nothing in her memory. Had he always been so sour and consumed by business? Was a happy father something she had ever seen? Well then, now was the time. It truly was Lucy's fondest wish for the trip— to be a happy family, all of them—and she was determined to keep that dream afloat.

7

ABBY

7:00 p.m. Wednesday, April 10, 1912

Abby took a bite of lamb with mint sauce and chewed, closing her eyes and savoring the flavor. She could not remember the last time she'd had food so warm and delicious, and served on shiny new china by a uniformed White Star Line steward no less! Master Miles would cringe to see the royal treatment she was receiving in the servants' dining salon. The only significant difference between the dining room where maids and valets ate and the regular second-class dining room was that the servants ate at long shared tables, and Abby's silver napkin ring had been stamped with the word *servant*.

"Now this is *food*!" Constance whispered, leaning

across the table. She speared half a roasted potato and stuffed it into her mouth. For a moment she was quiet while she chewed, but the silence did not last long. "Can you imagine what they're serving in first class?" she asked through her bite.

Abby shook her head. She hadn't even known Constance for a day, but that was long enough to know the girl could keep up both sides of a conversation with very little encouragement. Besides, before Abby could tell Constance what she knew about the first-class dining, the housemaid had moved on to other things. She was scanning the servants' hall, peering at each man in turn.

"Too old. Too young. Too shy." Her eyes traveled down the long table on the other side of the room. "Is that a wedding ring?" she asked aloud, squinting. "Not a single candidate in here," she said with a dramatic sigh, then brightened. "But maybe some of the ship's officers are single . . ." She waggled her eyebrows at Abby before taking another large bite.

Abby smiled down at her plate. She liked Constance in spite of herself, and in spite of the challenges having a roommate created with Felix. It wasn't easy keeping her brother a secret in their shared berth.

Taking advantage of Constance's chewing, Abby inter-
jected in the girl's endless monologue. "Did you hear we're
taking on more passengers here in France?" she asked. The
ship was docked off the coast of Cherbourg to load passengers and mail. "Maybe your future husband is amongst them,"
she added in a teasing tone. "He could be boarding right this
moment!"

Constance's eyebrows darted upward. "Well, perhaps
we should go greet him!" she declared, lurching to her feet.
But a moment later she was scowling down at Abby. "Oh,
you've barely had a bite," she pouted. It was true—Abby's
plate was more than half-full.

"It's perfectly all right. You go on," Abby said. "I want
to stay for pudding anyway."

Constance pushed in her chair and leaned down to
whisper in Abby's ear. "Ooh, wait. Perhaps I was wrong
about there not being any candidates in here. That there is a
lad with promise!" Candace pointed toward a steward clear
ing plates—the same boy who had heard her talking to Felix
through her cabin door! He looked up and caught both girls
staring directly at him.

Abby tried to look away before the steward could recognize her, to no avail. They locked eyes. The steward began

to smile, but Abby pulled her gaze away and concentrated on her potatoes.

"If only he were a bit older," Constance sighed, unaware of Abby's rosy cheeks. "Or I were a bit younger . . ." She continued to talk to herself as she headed out of the dining room.

Abby kept her eyes cast down until Constance and the steward were both gone. Then, discretely, she opened the linen napkin in her lap and loaded it with as much of the food left on her plate as she could. She would have relished eating every bite of the delicious dinner herself, but the thought of the hungry boy waiting in her cabin kept her from doing so. When she'd squirreled everything away, she tied the ends of the napkin together and tucked the makeshift sack of food into the waistband of her skirt. She held her breath as she made her way out of the dining room and didn't let it out until she reached her cabin.

ISABELLA

4:00 a.m. Thursday, April 11, 1912

Isabella turned in her bunk to face the wall of her dark third-class quarters. She could hear the heavy sleep breathing of her bunkmates—a Swedish mother and her four children—and also the ship's engines, because the cabin was situated on a lower deck in the stern of the ship. With its freshly painted paneled walls and spotless linoleum floor, their berth was much nicer than the tiny apartment she'd shared with her parents. Isabella had never slept on linens as crisp and white as those provided by the White Star Line. The cotton blankets were even woven with the company's logo!

Unfortunately, the beautiful new bedding did nothing to help Isabella sleep, and the fine cabin did not assuage her feelings of hopelessness and loss. Living with a family in tight quarters—two bunks were stacked against three of the walls—was heartbreaking. The chatter and camaraderie of the five relations only made her feel more alone.

Silent tears leaked from Isabella's eyes and soaked into her pillow. She wanted to sleep, to forget that she was on a huge boat in an even bigger ocean going to a country she'd never seen. Everyone she came in contact with would be a stranger!

My parents needed to be rid of me, she thought, racking her brain for the reason they had sent her away. But it didn't sound right, not even in her mind. She had done all that she could to not be a burden, to help her family—especially after the strike. She stayed home from school to do chores. She took in mending and helped her mother with the wash when her hands got too red and raw from the lye soap. Even working together, their efforts only resulted in a few pennies—perhaps it was not enough to make a difference.

So many questions swirled in her head. One loomed larger than the rest. *What will become of me in America?*

Slipping her hand underneath her pillow, Isabella touched the sealed letter her mother had pressed into her hands at the dock. The one she had promised not to open for six more days.

Six days. An eternity.

Isabella was not going to sleep. She rolled over again, got out of her bunk, and dressed as silently as she could. The Swedish family slept on as Isabella quietly unlatched the door and made her way through the maze of corridors and stairways to the third-class areas on the upper decks of the ship.

Out on the poop deck, the sky was changing color from inky black to peachy gray. Soon the sun would peek over the endless ocean horizon.

Isabella gazed out, leaning on the ship rail for support. Two nights with hardly any sleep had left her a bit weak. Clutching the letter in both hands, she could not keep from trembling. She'd promised she would not open it . . . not until they neared New York. But the letter was her only hope for answers, and her questions were torture. Besides, she reasoned, her mother was not here . . . she would never even know that Isabella had broken her promise.

Sliding a shaky finger under the flap of the envelope, she broke the seal. Inside were two documents: a letter in her mother's faltering hand, and another singed piece of paper folded behind it.

Isabella heard her mother's voice in her head as she slowly read . . .

My Dearest Daughter,

I never thought the day would come when I would have to tell you this, for although you are the heart of my heart and will forever be my darling daughter, you were not born to me and your father. It has been our greatest honor and duty to raise you as our dear child. We had no offspring of our own and adopted you when you were just a few days old.

In these difficult times, we wondered if we had done you a disservice, as we cannot provide the education, luxuries, or pleasures in life that you deserve. You are a clever girl, Isabella, strong and smart. With opportunities you will surely go far. It breaks my heart that Francis and I are unable to give you those opportunities.

When a lady's maid appeared at our doorstep with news, and proof of your birth parents, that truth became even more apparent. You are the daughter of Phillip and Elisabeth Miles. They are people of means, and the parents who can grant you the life that we cannot. Your father and I were not sure how to share this news with you, or with the Miles family. When we found out that they had booked passage aboard Titanic to travel to America, we knew that we needed to make sure you sailed with them.

Find them, dear girl. Tell them who you are. They could not be so callous as to turn you away. In America you can become what you never could here, shackled by your old and ailing parents. (I hope you do not mind that I call us that, this last time.) Our future is uncertain and bleak and it is this harsh future that we release you from. Please know we love you and want only the best for you and your future.

Your loving Mama and Papa

Isabella stared down at the letter, her tears falling onto the parchment. She couldn't believe her own eyes. For several moments all she could do was sob. Then, with quaking shoulders, she looked at the second singed document. Though one corner was completely burned away, she was able to read several lines: Certificate of Registry of Birth. County of London. Isabel Miles, born on the ninth day of September, 1899, to Phillip Miles and Elisabeth Miles.

Could it be true? It has to be! It was the only answer Isabella had, but it brought many new questions. She drew a ragged breath. She was not who she thought she was . . .

Isabella longed for the comfort of her mother—the only one she had ever known—Ruth James. She clutched the birth certificate to her chest and stared out at the gray dawn. She was farther from her home than she'd ever been, but they were not yet on the open ocean. Could she stow away on one of the tenders bringing mail and passengers to the *Titanic* from Queenstown? How difficult would it be to get back to land undetected? To find her way home?

It was more than a little daunting to think of getting off the boat in Ireland. Isabella had no idea how to get back to London from there, nor did she have the money to do so. Besides, if she were to disembark, her parents' investment—their entire savings—would be wasted. Isabella swallowed a sob. The choice had already been made. She had to stay on board.

"Are you all right there, miss?" a passing crewman asked on his deck rounds.

Isabella nodded and the crewman hurried on in the chilly morning air. She stuffed the letter back into the envelope and the envelope back into her pocket. She had to gather her wits and her fortitude. She had to reach for the bright future her parents envisioned for her—even if she couldn't envision it for herself.

Phillip and Elisabeth Miles were her real parents, and they were on board the *Titanic*.

Her future was in their hands.

9

LUCY

9:30 a.m. Thursday, April 11, 1912

"Let's just take a little stroll," Lucy suggested when she and her mother had finished their breakfast. Well, *she* had eaten breakfast . . . her mother had only poked disinterestedly at the food Abigail had brought to their rooms on a tray. But Lucy had a full belly and was eager to explore the ship. Yesterday's tour, cut short by her mother's desire to rest, had only skimmed the *Titanic*'s surface. Lucy hadn't yet seen the Turkish bath, the salons, the gymnasium, or had a chance to relax in a lounge chair on one of the first-class promenades.

She folded her napkin and stood up. "I'm sure some fresh air will do us all good." She smiled in the direction of her father, who had his head buried in a newspaper. "Father, would you like to come with us?" she asked. "There are so many society people on board. Perhaps we will run into someone you know—maybe a business associate," she added more boldly when he did not respond.

Phillip thrust the paper aside and glared at Lucy. "Don't be ridiculous," he said. "We don't know anyone on board."

Elisabeth dabbed her mouth with her napkin and folded it into a neat triangle. "Well, there *was* that man who was calling to you from the dock yesterday," she said mildly. "Perhaps he was boarding."

"Don't be ridiculous!" Phillip repeated more sharply. "There was no man."

Elisabeth set her napkin across her plate and looked at her husband quizzically. "Phillip, he was calling your name," she insisted, sitting up taller.

Lucy's father scowled. "I think your nerves are making you delusional again, Elisabeth," he said. "Perhaps we should take you to the ship's doctor. I've heard Dr. O'Loughlin is a fine surgeon. Maybe *he* will have a tonic that will succeed in keeping you rational."

Lucy saw her mother shrink back and felt a flash of anger. Her father could be so cruel! And her mother was not delusional—she'd seen the man on the dock, too! She heard him call her father's name, clear as anything. Lucy opened her mouth to tell her father this, but he cut her off before she could start.

"Don't you go agreeing with your mother just to make her feel better, Lucy," he said crossly. Lucy recognized his tone and knew at once what it meant. If she pressed he would begin to shout, further upsetting her mother. Her mother would then take to her bed for the rest of the day and possibly the rest of the crossing. She'd seen him disregard his wife before. He frequently brushed off her thoughts and requests like annoyances, a habit Lucy attributed to stress over his business dealings. But there was no denying that he was being especially insensitive now. Nevertheless, she sighed quietly and held her tongue. The last thing she wanted on their *Titanic* holiday was a row.

"I suppose I could have been mistaken," Lucy said, finding herself unwilling to fully back down.

Her father nodded curtly, slapped his folded newspaper onto the settee, and stood. "Perhaps, since you aren't feeling well, you should spend the day inside," he suggested, addressing his wife without looking at her. He leaned in and gave Lucy a kiss on the forehead. Lucy said nothing as she watched her father gather his coat and walk brusquely away from them, nearly colliding with Abigail, who was coming through the doorway that connected the sitting room and bedrooms with her arms full of hats and coats.

"You're forever in the way!" he barked, scowling at the maid. "And they won't be needing those. You should be clearing the dishes!" Brushing her aside, he strode out of the stateroom.

Lucy forced a smile for the startled girl. She was glad to see her. Abigail was certainly better company than her sour father.

"He's in a mood, isn't he?" Abigail said, nodding toward the closed door.

Lucy blinked in surprise. Abigail's mother, O'Rourke, never would have uttered a word against her master—she wouldn't have raised an eyebrow! But the younger maid spoke the truth—her father *was* in a mood. Permanently, it seemed!

"Never mind him. It's a glorious morning and I think the two of you should take in some fresh sea air. I've heard that the covered promenade on A deck is especially lovely, and some time outside will no doubt do you heaps of good," Abigail said as she offered up the hats and coats.

Lucy's heart swelled with gratitude as her mother stood and let Abigail help her into her overcoat. "Yes," she said. "I believe a walk and some air will do us all good."

10

ABBY

10:00 a.m. Thursday, April 11, 1912

"I'll join you on deck as soon as I've tidied up," Abby told Mistress Elisabeth and Miss Lucy. "I'm afraid I've got a few things left to do."

Elisabeth nodded. "We will have a nice stroll and then perhaps a rest on the covered promenade," she said. "When you've finished, you can look for us there."

Abby fiddled with her skirt nervously. "I'll meet you just as soon as I can, ma'am," she said as she turned away. She stacked the plates and cups onto the White Star Line tray, taking notice of Mistress Miles's untouched food. She draped a napkin across the scones, butter, jam, and fruit and listened for the stateroom door to close. The uneaten breakfast would be perfect for Felix—she hadn't managed to get anything out of the servants' dining room earlier, and her poor brother was probably starving! He was always starving.

As soon as the door latched and her employers were off, Abby wrapped the food in a napkin. She gathered the heavy silver warming trays and their lids, balancing them carefully, and hurried to return them to the serving rooms. She returned to the stateroom just as quickly, rushing to fetch the food she'd set aside before anyone happened upon it. She was jumpy as a rabbit as she started down the maze of passages once more to deliver Felix's breakfast. Though she looked around anxiously as she went, Abby did not see Miss Lucy until she was descending toward B deck. A moment later she heard her name being called. "Abigail!"

Abby gulped and quickly hid the napkin of food under her apron.

"Where are you off to?" Miss Lucy asked, peering at her from the top stair. "We're up here on the promenade as you suggested."

Abby flushed. "So sorry, Miss. I just returned the food

trays and . . . I . . . well, this ship is so large it has me all topsy-turvy. I think I got a bit lost."

Miss Lucy smiled. "It can be confusing," she admitted, holding out her coat. "It's warmer out than I expected, so I won't be needing this," she said. "Would you mind taking it back to the stateroom?"

Abby nodded and took the heavy outer garment with one hand, holding it to hide the lump under her apron. "Of course not, Miss."

"Thank you. And please feel free to leave a bit of the work for later if it means you can join us for a wander? Mother so enjoys your company, and it would be good to get more familiar with the ship."

Abby was pleased by the comment but displeased by the pastry crumbs she saw rubbing from her fingers onto the fine wool of the green overcoat. "Of course, Miss. Thank you, Miss." She sounded like a dolt, but she would say anything to get Miss Lucy to go back to her mother so she could deliver Felix's manhandled breakfast. His stomach was probably growling like a bear's.

Abby watched Miss Lucy depart, waiting until she turned a corner. Then she spun around and hurried past the ornately carved clock and down the three flights of the Grand Staircase to D deck.

As she rushed toward her cabin, Abby crossed her fingers and said a silent prayer that Constance was out watching passengers arrive from Queenstown, Ireland, where they had moored—the last stop to take on mail and passengers before heading out on the long crossing. She was anxious for Constance's absence, though not because her berthmate loved to prattle on and on . . . and on. Abby was, in fact, grateful for her rambling roommate—Constance's constant talk helped to mask Felix's noise. Their first night on board had been cramped and stuffy in the upper bunk with the heavy curtain drawn tight. Sharing her pillow with a pair of kicking feet was no picnic, either, but they'd survived.

Before she left to get breakfast and dress Lucy and Elisabeth, she'd whispered to Felix to stay put and stay quiet. He'd rolled over and pointed toward his mouth to indicate that he was hungry. Of course.

"I'll be back with food as soon as I can," she'd said softly, but that was well over two hours ago.

She was out of breath as she pushed open the door to cabin D22. "I've got scones, Felix," she said once she'd made certain Constance was gone. The curtain was still drawn around the upper bunk. Perhaps Felix had stretched out and slept on. She set the coat down on the long sofa and brushed the crumbs off before pulling aside the curtain. "Wake up, Fe—? The words evaporated and Abby stood with her mouth open.

The bunk was empty!

"Felix?" she called, quickly scanning the rest of her quarters. "Felix!"

There was no answer, and no Felix!

Worry crawled up Abby's spine like a parade of spiders. If Felix were discovered, they'd be thrown off the boat in Queenstown—or worse!

Abby paced in front of the washbasin. What on earth made her think she could keep her feisty little brother in a single room for an entire week? She hadn't even managed a full day! She looked up and caught her reflection in the mirror. It was the reflection of a young girl in far, far over her head. Tears sprang to her eyes and she watched her chin begin to quiver. She was doing her best, but her best would never be enough to fill her mother's capable shoes. Abby's legs suddenly felt weak, as if she might actually fall down. She missed her mother so much!

The girl in the mirror wanted her mother back, and also wanted answers. She'd jumped so quickly into her mother's shoes that she hadn't had time to wonder how or why her mother had died so suddenly.

Perhaps Abby should not have accepted the job Master Miles offered. Everything had happened at once. Phillip Miles informed her of her mother's passing and offered Abby her mother's position in the same meeting (after making it quite clear he was doing her a grand favor taking on an orphan with no prospects). She'd been stunned, unable to think. Was that manipulation on Master Miles's part? It seemed entirely possible. Though her mother loved Mistress Elisabeth and Miss Lucy, she had also confided in Abby that she did not like or trust Master Miles—a feeling that seemed to have intensified shortly before she died.

Abby remembered finding her mother sitting up late one night just a few weeks before she disappeared. She had come into their tiny sitting room to spend a bit of quiet time together, as they liked to do after Felix was asleep. But that night Maggie O'Rourke was preoccupied. She was sitting very still, staring at a scorched piece of paper and talking to herself.

"Mama?" Abby had called softly.

Maggie had looked up then, as if she were coming out of a trance. She had blinked at Abby and opened her arms wide. She'd embraced her tightly, muttering in Abby's ear about never giving her up. It was such a strange thing to say—her mother was not a worrier, even after her father passed away. Maggie O'Rourke was quick to laugh, and first to count her blessings. Hearing her sound so frightened had made Abby feel unsettled. She'd hugged her mother back extra tightly. "You won't ever have to give me up," Abby had said, and it was true.

It would be Abby and Felix who'd be forced to give up their mother. Less than a month later she was lost to them forever.

The truth was that even if she'd been thinking clearly, Abby did not have a choice about Master Miles's offer. She had to care for her brother. She had to care for herself. She was both mother and sister now. As she gazed at the grief-stricken, angry girl looking back at her, Abby realized that Master Miles must have known that she could not refuse. She forced herself to stand taller.

"Don't worry, Mama. We will make it to America," she vowed. She felt for her mother's savings, which were tied in a small bundle around her waist. It wasn't much, but it would give them a start. In America she would send Felix to school. She would work as a maid, or doing laundry, or in one of the factories that were popping up in New York. She and her brother would build a new life . . .

But first she had to find him.

11

ISABELLA

10:30 a.m. Thursday, April 11, 1912

Isabella pulled her best dress—a gray brocade her mother had taken in as washing that was never retrieved—from her carpetbag. She smoothed it with her small hands, noting the worn fabric and wrinkles. By far the finest dress she had ever owned, it was also tired—as tired as she was, she realized woefully.

Never mind, she told herself. If she was going to search for Phillip Miles—in the areas of the ship where her well-to-do biological father might actually *be*—she had to present herself differently. Third-class passengers were not permitted to mingle in first- or even second-class areas.

She tried not to think too much about what she was

attempting, or what it would require, as she washed as best she could over the small sink in her berth. As lovely and new as the accommodations on the *Titanic* were, the entire third class only had two bathtubs! Fortunately, Isabella was practiced at bathing without a tub, and her mother had had the good sense to pack a small scrap of soap. It was also fortunate that the Swedish family she shared her cabin with was already on the steerage deck at the stern, so she didn't have to contend with curious eyes watching her twist and pin her hair up and back, doing her best to imitate the sophisticated styles she'd seen on the streets of London.

After working for nearly an hour, Isabella looked herself over in the mirror. She didn't have any jewelry, and her hair was unwashed. Her appearance was far from first class, but would have to do. She steeled herself with a deep breath, straightened her shoulders, and left the cabin.

Isabella practiced holding her head high as she made her way through the maze of stairs and passageways up to the gates to the second-class boat decks. A young male passenger in britches tipped his hat as she passed, letting out a low whistle. He was probably mocking her for taking on airs. She ignored him, but her flushing cheeks did not.

You musn't react to anything, she told herself as she approached the doors leading out of steerage. *You must appear calm no matter what.* Though not locked, the gates were intended to keep third-class passengers in third class. Isabella's heart hammered in her chest as she pressed herself against the wall around the corner from a gate and waited for an opportunity to slip past the crewman on duty.

Luck was on her side, for this particular crewman was busy talking to another passenger. Dressed in dirty work pants and a wrinkled button-down shirt, the large man holding the crewman's attention had an angry-looking scar on his left cheek and a frustrated lilt to his voice.

The steward looked the man up and down. "I'm sorry, but you're not allowed beyond this point—those areas can only be accessed by first- and second-class passengers."

"I've got some business with someone in first class," the man said.

"If you write a message I might be able to deliver it for you . . . How badly do you need it delivered?" the guard asked in a knowing tone.

"I don't have any money to give you, but I'm telling you, this is urgent," the man said, his hands balling into fists.

"And I'm telling you that I *might* be able to get a message through . . . if the price is right."

The scarred man raised his hand and Isabella stepped back for a moment, worried that the conversation was about to come to blows.

The guard threw back his shoulders and shifted away from Isabella, circling the man. His hands were also raised, and when his back was turned Isabella saw her chance.

"You're not allowed through here, *sir*," the guard repeated as Isabella slipped by the both of them and scurried up the stairs.

....

The third-class deck, the one Isabella stood on when she'd learned she was not really Isabella James, was at the noisy rear of the ship and downwind of the massive smokestacks. The second-class promenade and boat deck were just forward of that and led to the first-class promenade, which was airier without the clutter of lifeboats. Since the *Titanic* was currently moored off Queenstown, Ireland, several bumboats were lined up at the *Titanic*'s stern, and merchants had come aboard to try and sell their wares to wealthy first-class passengers. This was lucky, for the commotion created by the merchants allowed Isabella to continue into first class undetected.

Her heart hammered in her chest as she strolled past the vocal merchants. They seemed almost desperate to sell their china dishes, crystal, and small souvenirs. She herself was enchanted by the ornate Irish lace. She watched as an obviously wealthy man purchased a beautiful shawl, delicate as a snowflake, and had to hide her gasp at the price. It was more than her father earned in a year!

No, a perfectly normal sum of money, she corrected herself, lifting her chin a bit higher and reminding herself who she was supposed to be.

Isabella nodded and smiled at the people she passed as she walked, just as she had seen ladies in London do on the rare occasions that she'd traveled with her mother to the more prosperous parts of the city. The passengers she passed appeared to accept her as one of their own, or at least didn't pay her any mind.

Even if the first-class areas hadn't been clearly demarcated by the presence of merchants, Isabella would have known that she was in first class in a heartbeat. The wealth was palpable. The women's pastel gowns were sumptuous, finely made, and heavy with beading. They all wore hats decorated with feathers and jeweled pins or carried parasols to shade their fair skin. The men were nearly as pale as the women in their tailored suits, high vests, and long coats. Everyone looked well polished, right down to their button-up boots. Isabella was suddenly grateful that the gown she wore was a bit too long, as it did an excellent job hiding her shabby everyday pair. She walked slowly and in what she hoped was a ladylike manner, searching the passengers' faces for . . . she didn't know quite what. Some feeling of recognition?

She'd never really considered that she didn't look much like the parents who'd raised her. She had always assumed that their ruddier complexions were due to their years of hard work outdoors, and though she didn't share it yet, she would. Her mother, Ruth, said Isabella's curls were a gift of the angels—an answer to her secret longings for curly hair when she was young. Isabella scanned the well-to-do crowd, discretely looking for features like her own.

Her instinct was to avoid the gazes of the wealthy passengers strolling the decks, but her intelligence told her just the opposite. She boldly made eye contact with a woman carrying a Pekinese, smiling at the pup's long ears and stubby, wrinkled snout. But when she looked into the face of the woman, her nose was wrinkled as well. Isabella flushed in embarrassment and quickened her pace.

Perhaps she was not passing in first class after all!

12

ABBY

11:30 a.m. Thursday, April 11, 1912

With Miss Lucy's coat folded over her arm, Abby frantically searched the second-class areas of the *Titanic* for her brother. Unfortunately, there were *several* second-class areas, and they weren't necessarily close together! She quickly walked the covered promenade on C deck, peeking in at the library where women sat reading or playing games while keeping a watchful eye on their children through the windows. She dashed down the red carpeted stairs—which, though not quite as grand as the staircase in first, were still very fine—to D deck, where the second-class dining room was, and arrived out of breath. Why oh why did she have to be on the biggest ship ever built?

Breathe, Abigail, she told herself. *You know perfectly well that panicking won't help.* She looked around the large and largely empty dining room and tried to think like a seven-year-old boy—what would Felix want to see most? She walked the boat deck on the very top of the ship, with its massive ventilation stacks and neatly tied lifeboats. She silently prayed that her daring little brother hadn't ventured down into the bowels of the ship to get a glimpse of the massive engines gulping coal, but the moment it occurred to her she knew that's exactly where he would go!

Don't imagine the worst, she scolded herself. But she couldn't help it. She lifted her skirts and hurried back to the stairs. She was certain there would be no access to the very bottom of the ship through first class, but she'd heard about the swimming pool, heated by the boilers, on F deck. If she could get to the pool, there might be access to the boilers nearby.

After several wrong turns Abby found the pool. She'd hardly gotten a glimpse inside the tiled, portal-windowed room that housed the heated saltwater bath when she was shooed along. It was the hour designated for women's swimming, however, so Felix wouldn't be there, and she'd seen enough to be certain that there was no entrance to the boilers.

She was tempted to give up, when she spotted a man in a dark worker's uniform turning down a narrow passage. She followed him into the crew's quarters and knew at once that she was on the right path. Men smudged with soot and dressed in filthy clothes were making their way through increasingly narrow corridors. The ship's boilers had to be fed day and night and the men, likely coming off their shift, were too tired to care about an out-of-place lady's maid. A few of them commented to one another, but Abby didn't understand what they said. And she could only think of one thing: finding Felix.

Following the trail of soot left by the workers, Abby descended a narrow stairwell. The very bottom of the boat was freezing cold near the outer hull, but when she got closer to the boilers she began to feel sweat beading on her forehead. How could anyone work in this heat for hours on end?

Up ahead, the stokers coming on shift knocked on a closed door. A moment later, it opened and Abby caught a glimpse of a massive boiler room. Five enormous, two-sided drums glowed fiery red inside while rugged-looking men shoveled in coal and carted wheelbarrows filled with the black fuel. The workers looked minuscule next to the huge furnaces! The man at the door gave Abby a funny look, but she already knew she would not be allowed in.

"I'm looking for my brother," she yelled over the deafening noise of the fire and the engines. The man looked confused for a moment, and Abby held out her hand to show Felix's height. "A boy!" she yelled again.

Suddenly understanding, the man grinned and nodded. Abby felt her heart swell with hope and hugged the coat she still held close to her chest. He had seen him! He pointed a dirty finger at the ceiling. Yes, Felix had come down, but he wasn't here any longer. He'd sent him back up. Oh, and after she'd come all this way!

Abby forced a small smile and nodded her thanks. She felt dizzy, and wasn't sure whether she should be relieved or worried. When she got her hands on her brother—*if* she got her hands on her brother—she would hug him and throttle him in equal measure. But she would have to halt her search for now and return to her duties, or risk drawing Miss Lucy and Mistress Elisabeth's suspicions . . . if she hadn't already.

By the time she got to the base of the Grand Staircase, she was so exhausted she decided to ride the electric elevators.

"Curse you, Felix O'Rourke!" she muttered as she hurried to the first-class promenade. She spied Miss Lucy and

Mistress Elisabeth almost immediately, relaxing on lounge chairs in the early afternoon sun. She was about to approach when she realized with annoyance that she was holding Miss Lucy's coat—the one she was supposed to take back to the still untidied stateroom! She could not be seen with it, or Miss Lucy would surely wonder what she'd been doing all this time. She folded it neatly over the back of a chair to retrieve later, not a moment before Miss Lucy spotted her.

"Abigail!" Miss Lucy called cheerfully.

Abby willed her pounding heart to be still and made her way over to the Miles women, relieved that they did not seem upset over her long absence. In fact they were in high spirits.

"You were so right, O'Rourke," Lady Miles announced as she approached. "All this fresh air and sunshine is making me feel renewed."

Abby smiled genuinely, but saw that Miss Lucy looked concerned.

"Should we go in for lunch?" she asked. "We mustn't overdo."

Lady Miles tugged the brim of her hat down to better shield her face from the sun and turned to her daughter. "No. Let's sit out for a bit longer," she said. "Perhaps we could even take our luncheon here in the open air."

"That's a wonderful idea, Mother!" Miss Lucy chimed. "Abigail, would you mind fetching us a tray?"

"Not at all," Abby replied, smiling and trying not to think of her tired legs and feet. Her mistresses were clearly enjoying themselves out on deck, as she'd hoped they would, and she wanted their pleasure to continue.

"I'd love a blanket if you can bring me one," Lady Elisabeth said. Abby found a tartan blanket on a nearby chair. As she was tucking it around her mistress's legs, she noted that it was finely woven, double-layered, and bore the emblematic White Star insignia. She was just finishing smoothing the woolen blanket into place when she spotted a familiar figure out of the corner of her eye.

Felix!

Abby's mouth gaped open. She quickly tried to position her body between her employers and her brother to block their view, but as she did her horror was amplified. Felix was not alone here in first class. He was being held up to the rail by the handsome steward—the same one who had caught her talking to her door not a day before!

13

ISABELLA

12:30 p.m. Thursday, April 11, 1912

After receiving several more disdainful looks from first-class passengers—mostly female—Isabella knew she needed to do more to disguise her shabby appearance. Though the first-class passengers were too well bred to *say* anything, their scowls spoke volumes. She was not one of them, and they knew it. She was looking for a place to hide when she spied an unattended overcoat draped over a lounge chair on the promenade. She bravely snatched it up and put it on, as if she'd left it there herself. She buttoned the coat up to the collar, hiding her dress entirely. The green wool was incredibly soft, and she stroked the collar absently, admiring it.

Don't be conspicuous! she reminded herself when she realized what she was doing. But it was difficult not to swoon over the finely made garment. She looked down at herself in the coat. By some stroke of luck it fit her remarkably well, and wrapped in its opulence she looked every bit as "first class" as the passengers around her. Certain she could fit in now, she felt herself relax a tiny bit.

Unfortunately, her relief was thwarted by the realization that she still had a significant problem. She'd already walked past dozens and dozens of passengers. She'd looked into their faces, peering at their chins and eyes for clues. Each one was a stranger. How, on such a massive ship carrying over one thousand passengers, would she ever find her birth parents? And even if she should locate them, how could she identify them? How would she know them? She had no photo, no information at all about what they looked like. All she had was her father's name. It wasn't as if the passengers had them stamped on their foreheads!

Perhaps I could ask a crewmember who he is, Isabella thought, then immediately dismissed the idea. Drawing further attention to herself would be unwise, and dangerous.

But the hopelessness of the search threatened to overwhelm her. The task that Ruth and Francis had set for her was impossible! Had they considered how she would actually find her birth parents, or had they just shoved her aboard the massive ship and hoped for the best?

Exhausted and disheartened, she sank onto a deck chair near the back of the boat.

Her eyes began to water from a combination of frustration and the acrid cigar smoke blowing out of the lounge windows.

I can't give up now, Isabella told herself. She heard her father's voice in her mind—the way he chuckled as he gave her advice. *You've got pluck, my Bella. Pluck and sense, and those two combined with hard work is all a person needs to make it in this world.* Only she was no longer in a world that she knew.

Closing her eyes for a moment and trying to locate the resolve she knew was inside her, Isabella heard another voice in her head. No, wait—this one was not in her head. Bits of conversation were wafting out of the first-class smoking room window above her, along with the clouds of smoke.

"That's quite a scheme you have going, Miles."

Isabella's ears pricked at the name. *Miles!* She sat upright and turned, feigning adjusting the buttons on her coat. She waited, but the man's voice she'd heard was now silent. Had she imagined those words? Had they come to her out of sheer desperation?

Rising slightly, Isabella stole a look through the glass. The room was empty save for a steward wiping tables at the far end and two men playing a game of cards at a table. Isabella recognized gambling when she saw it. Though Francis James did not partake, she knew that many men did.

The gentlemen's faces were hidden in shadow, but Isabella could see that one man had silver hair, the other dark curls. The heavy oak table where they played was covered with empty glasses and cards. It was barely past lunchtime, and yet Isabella suspected that both men were a bit drunk given the volume of their voices.

The dark-haired man's slurred speech confirmed her suspicions. "Why, that's just the beginning," he said boastfully. "I will be leaving the unsuspecting Lady Elisabeth with her brother in America—preferably locked in a sanatorium, and paid for by said American brother. The poor man won't know what's hit him by the time I am sailing back to London, free as a bird. A wealthy bird, I might add . . ." He trailed off, staring at the cards in his hand. Isabella's mind reeled. The dark-haired man was Phillip Miles . . . her father!

"And what of your daughter?" the silver-haired man asked, sounding a bit incredulous. Whether he was disgusted by or disbelieving of Miles's plan, Isabella could not be sure. She herself was aghast. *Daughter? Does he know I'm on board?*

"Why, she will stay in America, too. Haven't you ever heard of boarding school?"

Isabella's jaw dropped as a fresh cloud of smoke and alcohol fumes wafted out of the window and into her nostrils. She felt undeniably ill and covered her mouth with her hand. How could this awful man possibly be her father?

She thought of Francis James, who had loved her and cared for her for as long as she could remember . . . a kind, gentle, hardworking man. She could hear his voice in her ear as if he were sitting next to her, see his warm smile. "They won't know what's struck them, I tell you," Phillip Miles bragged to his companion as they stood to leave.

"That's quite a scheme, Old Man," the silver-haired gentleman said. He shook his head as if he hadn't believed a word. "If only I had thought if it myself before I footed the bill for my daughter's wedding!"

Both men laughed, but only one was joking.

Isabella started when she realized that they were exiting

the smoking room and coming her way. A moment later they passed directly by her chair! She froze, trying not to draw their attention, but could not stop herself from staring. She looked Phillip Miles right in the face, hoping she would see some proof that the fiend was *not* her father. But what she saw confirmed her fears. They shared the same dark curls, the same wide-set hazel eyes. Only *his* eyes were cruel.

"If I were a caring man, I might actually feel sorry for them. They are just women, after all," Phillip Miles said as he passed. He laughed alone.

A strong and sudden urge to flee overtook Isabella. She struggled upward, tripping over her own feet and the chair.

"Do you need assistance, young lady?" the gray-haired man asked, reaching out a hand.

"N-no thank you," Isabella replied while her newfound father smirked unkindly. She ducked her head and hurried away, Phillip Miles's snickers echoing in her ears.

"What's gotten into her? You'd think she'd seen a ghost," he said, still chortling at her distress.

Isabella held herself upright, walking quickly and blinking back horrified tears as she fled. *That man can*not *be my father!* she told herself over and over. If this was the person she needed to depend on, she wouldn't! She'd rather beg in the streets or work in the poorhouse than accept anything from someone so awful.

It wasn't until she was down on D deck that she halted, remembering one of the things Phillip Miles had said. He had spoken of a daughter, but did not know that she, Isabella, existed. That could only mean one thing.

Isabella had a sister.

14

ABBY

1:00 p.m. Thursday, April 11, 1912

"I'll get you a tray at once!" Abby blurted, already turning to leave. She was not sure if Miss Lucy and Mistress Elisabeth would recognize Felix, but she *was* sure that she couldn't take the chance.

Glancing back to ensure her employers weren't watching her, and silently thanking the other passengers between them and the rail for blocking their view, she strode up to the steward who stood laughing with her brother.

"What do you think you are *doing*?" she hissed, wondering which of them she was addressing.

"Abby!" Felix lit up at the sight of his sister. He turned and reached his arms out for a hug.

Abby deflected the embrace and put her finger to her lips to shush him.

"Oh, it's Abby, is it? I was wondering what your name might be . . ." The steward smiled his devastating smile, which, thanks to her anger, Abby was able to ignore out of hand.

Taking in her stern expression, the steward quickly reshaped his smile into an expression of dutiful obedience. He set Felix firmly on the deck. "We were just watching them load the mail on and off the tenders," he said sheepishly. "No harm done."

"That's not all! We've been all over the ship!" Felix prattled excitedly to his sister. "Jasper even showed me the boiler—"

Abby wasn't listening. Ignoring Jasper altogether, she yanked Felix by the arm and dragged him toward the second-class staircase. But she neglected to look where she was going, and collided with a young girl headed in the same direction.

"Oh!" the girl exclaimed, startled. Both girls stumbled back. Jasper caught Abby easily, and she jerked away from him, glaring.

"Pardon me—I'm so sorry!" the girl stumbled over her

apology. Abby looked the girl up and down and her surprise turned to utter shock. The girl was wearing Miss Lucy's coat . . . the one she herself had set down just a few moments before!

"Wh-where did you get that coat?" Abby demanded, unable to keep the accusation out of her voice.

Jasper raised an eyebrow, and Abby knew what he was thinking. A maid accusing someone in first class of stealing, even a younger girl, was unheard of.

The girl stepped back, wrapping the coat more tightly around her thin frame. "I . . . I . . ." she mumbled. Then she straightened and looked Abby in the eye. Abby gazed back at the girl, feeling as if she had seen her somewhere before. But how was that possible?

"In London, of course," the girl finally replied. Turning on her heel, she strode quickly back the way she'd come.

15

ABBY

1:15 p.m. Thursday, April 11, 1912

Abby watched the girl go, a queasy feeling growing in the pit of her stomach. Why did she seem so familiar? Had Abby seen her when they were boarding?

Never mind, she told herself, returning her attention to Felix and the steward, who had located his handsome smile and was wearing it boldly. She threw a furtive glance back toward Miss Lucy and Mistress Elisabeth, who were resting on deck with their eyes closed, oblivious to the scene being played out before them. *Thank goodness.*

Abby reached for her brother's hand. She had to get him out of here right away! "You're coming with me," she said through clenched teeth. "Right this minute!" She hustled him down the stairs and back toward their cabin in silence. Inside, she was shouting at the top of her lungs.

When they finally reached D deck, Abby pulled Felix around a corner and, unable to contain her anger a moment longer, stopped and drew up close to the boy's face.

"What on earth were you thinking, Felix O'Rourke?" she cried, balling her hands into fists and beginning to pace. Pacing wasn't ladylike, she knew, nor was raging, or making fists, but she didn't have the time or the patience to be dainty!

"Do you even understand the danger we are in? Master Miles is not a nice man! He wanted to send you to a workhouse! If the family sees you . . . I . . ."

Felix blinked several times before his eyes filled with tears. "He wanted to send me to a workhouse?" His voice came out like the tiny mew of a newborn kitten, and Abby instantly felt awful. Her mother did not lose her temper like this. She didn't yell like this. She didn't frighten her children . . . ever.

Overflowing with guilt, she tugged his hand. "Oh, come on," she said. "Let's just get you to our cabin." She tried to pull him forward, but he tugged back.

"It's this way," Felix said.

Abby stopped. Was it possible that after just a few hours of freedom her little brother knew his way around the ship better than she?

"He's right," came a familiar voice. Jasper! Was he following them? "It's faster to go this way," the steward said gently.

Abby's eyes went round. Jasper had been spying. He'd probably heard every word she'd said and could turn them in at any moment! Their terrible secret was out.

The panic must have shown on her face, because Jasper stepped closer and quietly said, "If you don't mind my saying, Miss Abby, you don't need to worry about me."

"That's right!" Felix agreed. "Jasper promised he won't tell anyone I'm a row-away."

Abby's breakfast started to rise in her stomach. *He knows everything.* Surely the steward would have to turn them in to the proper on-ship authorities.

"Stowaway," Jasper corrected Felix gently, turning his large brown eyes on Abby. "And it's true, your secret is safe with me," he said earnestly. "On my parents' graves. There is plenty of room on this ship for everyone."

Abby's heart gave a little leap. Not only was he on their side, he was also an orphan! A pair of passengers passed by and she realized that they were still in a public corridor. She so wanted to believe she could trust this steward. But even if she decided she could, it only solved one of her problems.

"Felix, lead us to our cabin," she instructed. Felix grinned and turned on his heel. A few minutes later they were standing outside D22.

"Wait right here," she said sternly to both of them, pressing a finger to her lips. She suspected that Constance was at lunch—the girl loved to eat almost as much as she loved to talk—but entered the cabin by herself to investigate properly. Satisfied that the cabin was empty, Abby yanked Felix and Jasper inside and latched the door.

There were a few things they needed to get straight . . . immediately.

16

LUCY

1:45 p.m. Thursday, April 11, 1912

I wonder what's taking Abigail so long . . . Lucy thought. The maid had practically run from the deck, but she'd promised to bring a tray of lunch, and Lucy didn't see her anywhere. She gazed at the calm waters, grateful for her mother's repose. Elisabeth Miles was stretched out on the chaise beside her, covered with a blanket, looking serene. It was almost laughable—for once her frazzled mother was relaxed, and their usually unflappable maid seemed rattled and out of sorts! Lucy's stomach gurgled and she looked down the deck hoping to see Abigail. But there were only other first-class passengers enjoying the mild weather.

As she watched a pair of young girls her age linger by the rail, she felt a pang of sadness. How she wished she could introduce herself and perhaps befriend them! She'd love nothing better than to spend time with other young women, but was inexorably tied to her ailing mother.

Enough pity! Lucy scolded herself. *You have nothing to complain about!* Still, she let out a small sigh as the girls shared a laugh and moved on.

The *Titanic* had just left Queenstown. The real passage was under way and they would not stop again until they reached New York. Lucy wanted to build on her mother's mood and newfound strength, but found herself worrying about her untouched breakfast and current lack of lunch, as it was getting late.

Lucy stood and raised a hand to her eyes, looking up and down the deck.

As she searched, she noticed a man who looked out of place walking quickly along the promenade. Dressed in work pants, boots, and a wrinkled button-down shirt, he didn't appear to be a first-class passenger, and when he turned and Lucy saw the scar running down his cheek she knew for certain that he wasn't. She felt the tingle of alarm and wondered what he was doing.

Lucy watched as the man searched the faces of the passengers he passed, her heartbeat quickening in her chest. She started to look around for a steward and was relieved to see one of the ship's officers approach the stranger. There was a brief exchange, and the officer took the man's arm. The scar-faced man shook him off angrily, then seemed to yield, allowing himself to be escorted away.

"What is it Lucy?" her mother asked, opening her eyes.

"Oh, it's nothing," Lucy fibbed. "I was just thinking I should have told Abigail to bring your tonic as well."

"Now, now, don't fuss." Elisabeth reached out to pat her daughter's hand and smiled. It was a smile Lucy loved and didn't see nearly often enough. She sat back down. She decided she was being silly and should simply enjoy her mother's good humor. Abby would be along soon enough.

"Besides, I stopped taking that tonic. It smells awful, and tastes even worse. It isn't working in any case—even your father has said so," Elisabeth added, still smiling.

"Oh, but—" Lucy stopped herself from saying that it was Father who insisted she drink the dreadful cure day after day. Her mother didn't need to be reminded of that fact, and Lucy liked it when her mother was defiant—particularly when it put her in such high spirits.

How many years had it been since Elisabeth was involved in London's Women's Social and Political Union? It seemed like ages ago and just last week all at once. Back then, when her mother was stronger, Lucy had loved accompanying her to the rallies to demand the vote for women. She found it exhilarating, especially when Elisabeth would lean down to whisper, "We're making history, Lucy. Always remember this."

Deeds not words. That was the rallying cry of the WSPU. When the arrests were made and the front pages of the paper were plastered with images of suffragettes, Lucy had felt proud. But her father claimed that what the women had done was foolhardy and dangerous. He had forbidden his wife from participating any longer. Her mother had argued, and her parents had both yelled, their angry voices echoing through the Miles home. But it hadn't stopped her mother from sneaking out the very next day with her pamphlets, pressing a finger to her lips and giving Lucy a wink behind her nurse's back. Lucy had loved the twinkle in her mother's eyes, even if she rarely saw it now.

It wasn't very long after that, around the time that a few of the suffragette leaders were imprisoned, that Elisabeth had started feeling poorly. Her energy slowly drained away.

Some days she stayed in bed until the afternoon, and some days she didn't get out of bed at all. There were doctor visits and fewer and fewer outings. Now and again, Elisabeth Miles would appear to be regaining her strength, but it never lasted for long.

Lucy's nurse, Potter, left the family, and her mother's maid, O'Rourke, became Lucy's maid, too. O'Rourke did what she could to entertain Lucy, but she had her hands full with her mother's flagging health. Soon both mother and daughter had become housebound, and Lucy rather restless. She missed the park. She missed lunches with friends. She missed the rallies—and most of all she missed her mother's spirit.

"Oh, Miss! I'm so sorry that took me so long. I get so turned around on this ship I hardly know which way is the sky!" Abigail set the tray down between Lucy and her mother and fanned her face for a moment, looking harried. She was every bit O'Rourke's daughter, but unlike her mother, the younger O'Rourke was not skilled at hiding her emotions.

"We've been fine," Lucy said to reassure her. "Haven't we, Mother?" She was glad Abigail had returned to pull her out of her memories, and bring some food at last.

"Here we are!"

A steward stepped up behind Abigail with another tray laden with tea and sandwiches. At the sound of his voice the maid nearly jumped out of her apron, coming close to upsetting both trays.

Lucy looked on, amused. She wasn't certain of what to make of Abigail's strange behavior.

"Oh!" Abigail gasped, putting a hand to her chest. "You gave me a start. Here. Set it here."

Lucy stole a look at her mother and saw she was watching the two servants with equal bemusement as they stepped around each other to fill the cups and plates. The always-smiling steward seemed quite familiar with their maid, and Lucy couldn't help but wonder if they hadn't met somewhere else on the ship, or if placing the lunch order had been something a little bit . . . more.

A sudden and surprising flash of emotion made Lucy look away. The feeling was sharp, and she blinked as she tried to understand it. *Am I envious of my mother's lady's maid?* It seemed preposterous. Abigail was under their employ. She was an orphan, poor as a church mouse, and had to care for her little brother in addition to her employment as a lady's maid. And yet . . . well, in many ways she had much more freedom than Lucy did—enough to have caught the fancy of a handsome boy! Lucy tried to squelch her feelings of self-pity. Though it was true, she wasn't likely to meet any beaus trapped in her house or bound to her mother's side, she could hardly complain about her lot in life. She shook her head and smiled at her own foolishness. It reminded her of the song about the girl in the gilded cage.

Taking a filled cup from the tray, Lucy extended it to her mother. "It's nice and hot," she said. Elisabeth took it and smiled. It was still quite warm in the sun, but in the shade of the overhang a chill was creeping in.

"Now what would you like to eat?" Lucy asked, eyeing the selection of sandwiches. Her mother, though, was not paying attention—she was watching the steward walk away. As was Abigail.

"Do you know that steward, O'Rourke?" Elisabeth inquired when the lad was out of earshot.

Abigail blushed and shook her head. "No, of course not, ma'am . . ." She busied herself with retucking a blanket around Lucy.

Lucy's mother took a sip of tea. "Pity," she murmured into her cup. "He's quite handsome."

Lucy struggled to swallow the bite of her sandwich

rather than cough it into her lap. "What did you say, Mother?" she asked.

Elisabeth Miles looked to her daughter, and then to her maid. "Oh, nothing . . ." she said, shaking her head. Her mouth was a flat line, but her eyes were laughing, and Lucy was quite sure she'd heard her correctly.

From the look on Abigail's face, Lucy surmised that the maid had heard her as well.

"O'Rourke, I think you may be getting too much sun. You look flushed," Elisabeth said.

Abigail raised a hand to her cheek, and Lucy, to save her from further embarrassment, set down her cup and hugged her own arms. "I think I'm getting a chill after all. Would you mind fetching my coat back?"

Lucy hoped the errand would give the poor maid a moment of relief.

But Abigail's eyes widened further, and she looked at Lucy strangely. The pink in her cheeks drained away until she was as pale as her apron. She stood stock-still for several seconds. Finally she responded.

"Of course, Miss," Abigail said as she backed away. "I'll just go and fetch it."

17

ISABELLA

2:00 p.m. Thursday, April 11, 1912

Unsure of where to go, Isabella had simply fled. She just kept going, moving forward, until she reached the *Titanic*'s bow on B deck and could not go a step farther—only the rails of the ship kept her from walking right out over the deep.

Isabella stared at the endless blue-gray of the Atlantic. Wind swept her hair back, loosening it from its careful knot, and pushing the wayward locks away from her temples. There was nothing ahead of the massive ship. Nothing but water and sky, and a future that was uncertain to say the least.

Isabella drew a quaking breath. The ocean was so beautiful, so impossible in its endlessness. And so terrifying. She shivered in the green wool coat, feeling more lost and alone than ever, and closed her eyes to the horizon.

Two faces haunted her waking daydream: Phillip Miles and the maid who had spotted her in the stolen coat. Of the two, Miles was by far the more frightening. She had never stopped to consider that her biological father might be a bad man. Nor, she realized, had her mama and papa when they put her on this ship. Their hopes, as well as her own, were dashed, but what had been done could not be undone. That ship had, quite literally, sailed.

Isabella thought of Francis James, the papa who had raised her. She thought of his rough hands and tender heart. The man from the smoking lounge didn't look as if he'd worked a hard day in his life. His hands were likely as smooth as the bald head of a new baby! It was his *heart* that was hard and callous. Isabella squeezed her closed eyes more tightly shut. She could never call a man like that *Father*! And yet she could not walk away, either.

Now her fate was bound to Phillip Miles—unless she chose to disembark in New York without ever letting on about the letter and her birth certificate. But how would a girl with no means, no family, and no connections make a life for herself in America?

A chill deeper than the bitter wind snaked its way inside the wool coat. She had more family than the dastardly Master Miles aboard the *Titanic*. She had a mother. She had a sister. And the terrible man she could never call *Father* was plotting against them both.

Isabella did not have to accept the charity of an evil man, but she did have to do what was right. She needed to find the rest of her biological family before they made port, and tell them what Phillip Miles was up to.

What if they are as awful as he is? The question came unbidden, and the very idea of it left her feeling even more alone. Still, it would not change her course of action. She knew what she must do in order to sleep at night, in order to be able to write to Mama and Papa and tell them all that had transpired.

Bella, look to the bright side. How many times had her mama lifted her chin and told her to have hope, reminded her that the darkest times were when it was most important to fan the flames?

Her eyes wide open, Isabella looked out at the Atlantic again. The sun glinted on the waves. She *had* always wanted a sister. That could be a bright side . . .

Ever since she was tiny she'd longed for a playmate, a

confidant, a best friend. The sisters who lived in the apartment downstairs, all three of them, bickered at times, but were closer than fingers in a mitten. Isabella had played with them occasionally, but it was as if the girls had their own language. And though Isabella wanted to understand it, what her heart really desired was someone of her own to share a secret language with. A sister.

You'll never be like sisters. The Miles family didn't want you when you were born . . . why would they want you now? A terrible voice deep in her consciousness trampled her hopes. *The Miles family gave you up. Threw you out.* "Like rubbish," Isabella told the wind.

Only, she would do them better. She would treat her biological mother and sister as people should be treated. She would find them. Warn them. Help them.

But first she would have to determine who—amongst the hundreds of first-class passengers—they were.

18

LUCY

5:30 p.m. Thursday, April 11, 1912

"Are you sure, Mother?" Lucy peered at her mother anxiously in the mirror while Abigail fastened her ruby necklace around her neck. It had already been a long, lovely day. After their late lunch on deck, they had spent some time writing postcards in the reading room. By Elisabeth Miles's standards the day had been quite exerting, and Lucy had thought her mother would stay in their stateroom until it was time for bed. But when the bugler played, alerting passengers that dinner would soon be served, Elisabeth had surprised Lucy again by insisting they dress for the dining room.

Lucy was delighted. It was only their second night, and she was anxious to meet other passengers. She hoped they might catch a glimpse of John Astor and his young bride, who had booked return passage to America after their European honeymoon, or Benjamin Guggenheim, one of several very wealthy Americans on board.

But now she worried at the signs of fatigue on her mother's face. "We could stay here tonight," she suggested gently.

"I'm fine," Elisabeth insisted, "and O'Rourke has fetched enough trays for one day." She managed a small smile and Lucy decided to drop the subject.

In the adjoining parlor room, Lucy's father paced anxiously. When Lucy and her mother emerged, instead of admiring their fine dresses, he snapped, "It's about time!"

"Here, Miss," Abigail handed Lucy a shawl as her father hurried them out of their suite and toward the reception for the dining.

Lucy's mother took her arm instead of her husband's, and Lucy noticed immediately that she was leaning rather heavily. She stood straighter, placed her hand over her mother's, and said a silent prayer that dinner would go well.

The reception room was already crowded with first-class diners dressed in the latest fashions and wearing sparkling jewels. Lucy was glad she'd chosen her peach chiffon with the contrasting underskirts. It was her best dress, but nonetheless paled beside the dresses of the other young women in the dining room. The empire-waist frocks in silks and velvets shimmered in the electric lights. One in particular, a deep lapis-blue gown with a short train, caught Lucy's eye and she wondered if she would be able to find something like it in New York. As she lost sight of the girl in blue, she realized she'd lost sight of her father as well and began to search for him in the milling crowd.

A steward near the door was announcing each guest as they entered the main room, and Lucy and her mother were drawing close. Lucy craned her neck, and spotted her father at last. He was already inside the dining room with a drink in his hand, and about to find a table without them! Lucy nudged her mother forward.

"Elisabeth Miles, and her daughter, Lucy," the steward pronounced. Lucy smiled and escorted her mother to the beautifully laid table her father was already standing beside. The seated diners smiled back, and the men stood politely. The family sat down and for a moment there was an awkward silence. Lucy wondered if her desire to get to know the other passengers was purely one-sided. She glanced at her mother, who was introducing herself politely to their tablemates, and admired the grand room.

The walls and ceiling were gleaming white with lovely patterning. Windows were set between the carved wall panels and lit from the outside to give the impression of being on land. Combined with the fine furnishings and polished table settings, it was difficult to believe they were on a ship.

Elisabeth turned away the first course of oysters and made small talk with their table companions, an American family traveling back to the States after a long vacation. The children, a boy and girl, were amusing themselves by playing some sort of game under the table that involved only their hands. They made faces at each other—not speaking—so they wouldn't be told to stop, and seemed to understand each other's every brow wag and nose squinch. They needn't have worried about getting caught. Their parents weren't paying a lick of attention.

"This tastes just like the salmon we had in Paris!" the children's mother exclaimed loudly over the poached fish. Her husband disagreed just as loudly, but with a hearty laugh, saying she was mistaken—they hadn't even had salmon since they left New York. Lucy smiled at the napkin in her lap and wondered if all Americans were loud, and whether her uncle's family would be as boisterous. She secretly hoped so.

It reminded her of the way her mother used to be—spirited and fun.

Suddenly an even louder, far less amused voice made Lucy stop chewing. On the other side of her mother, her father was engaged in conversation with an older gentleman, and the conversation appeared to be taking a turn.

"That's preposterous," her father boomed.

The man sitting across from him lowered his voice, but not so much that Lucy could not hear. "I am simply asking that you do the honorable thing and give me what you owe."

"All is fair in love and war . . . and cards," her father replied. "I'm just surprised to learn that you are a sore loser."

"Isn't this delicious?" Lucy asked, her voice pitched louder than usual in an attempt to distract attention from the arguing men. It was no use, however. The men's voices grew louder and soon her father was practically shouting.

"I owe you nothing!" he bellowed.

"That's a lie," the man insisted. "I suppose I should have known better than to play cards with a man who doesn't repay his debts!"

A sudden knot in her abdomen made Lucy's stomach clench. What was this man saying?

People were staring . . . or trying hard not to. Lucy stood to excuse herself and her mother before things escalated further. Out of the corner of her eye she saw the steward who had announced their arrival make his way past the waiters toward the men, likely in an effort to quell the disturbance.

It was far too late. The man across from her father stood up abruptly and tossed his napkin onto his plate. "I've heard enough of your lies and your vulgar boasting, Miles!" he admonished Lucy's father.

Lucy's mother did not have to be coaxed into making a hasty exit. She, too, pushed back her chair. "Please excuse us," she said softly. "I'm afraid I haven't much appetite."

That was an understatement. Lucy had lost her appetite as well. Leading her mother by the arm, she determinedly looked straight ahead and ignored the stares as they made their way to the exit. When she paused to get her shawl and her mother's coat from the attendant, the dining room was quiet, but the damage had been done.

When they were safe inside their stateroom, Elisabeth sank onto the sofa and closed her eyes. *Probably trying to shut out the awful image of Father causing a ruckus!* Lucy thought. She wished she could dispel her own anger so calmly. She paced the room with her hands clenched into fists, feeling like a volcano about to erupt. Her father with his surly moods, argumentative nature, and bad habits had already managed to blot the family's reputation on board, and they'd barely lost sight of land. Was it like this at home, too? Lucy had very little knowledge her father's business relationships in London, but could not escape the sinking feeling she had now. The rest of the voyage would undoubtedly be full of stares and clucking tongues. It was humiliating! Just the thought of going back into the dining room was more than she could bear.

"I'm going to get some air!" Lucy said suddenly. Abigail would be there soon to help her mother dress for bed, and Lucy had to do something to keep from exploding. She went to her wardrobe in search of her warm green coat. Not seeing it, she pulled her blue coat off its hanger and tossed it over her shoulders, anxious to be outside.

Why does he do this? Lucy wondered as she hurried toward the promenade. She reconsidered what she knew of him as a businessman. He had a reputation as a hard man—and certainly had a stable of people who worked with him regardless of his demeanor—but did he have to be so . . . unlikeable?

Bursting out of the doors, Lucy drew a deep breath. The cold evening air felt good in her lungs. She took another slow inhale, longing to let it out in a scream. After several more breaths she stopped shaking and began, at last, to feel normal. But as her anger cooled, the night's chill set in. Lucy pulled up her collar and shivered in her blue coat. She wished she'd been able to locate the warmer one, but she wasn't ready to go back inside. Not yet.

Almost as soon as she'd wished for her green coat she saw a girl walking toward her wearing a coat of exactly the same shade and style. As the girl drew closer Lucy could not help but stare. It wasn't a *similar* green coat—it was *her* green coat!

The girl was strolling alone and behaving oddly, peering too long into the face of each person she passed. Lucy grasped the ship rail as she drew closer and the girl turned to give her the same odd stare. They locked eyes and Lucy felt a jolt, like electricity, course through her. She opened her mouth to say something . . . but couldn't.

The girl appeared stunned as well. She missed a step and then picked up her pace, averting her eyes and hurrying past Lucy without a word. Lucy was dumbfounded. She let the girl walk on for several paces and then turned to follow.

What on earth is she doing with my coat?

Now that she thought about it, Abigail had acted strangely earlier, bringing her blue coat when she'd asked for the green one. Had the maid given her coat away? Sold it? Did Abigail know this girl?

The departing girl walked faster and faster, and then, without turning back, darted into the second-class staircase and began to descend. Lucy paused. She hadn't seen much of second class, but it was no surprise that a girl with a stolen coat was not traveling in first. She followed her down to C deck, and then D, and then lost sight of her completely in a sudden press of people.

Lucy turned in a slow circle. Second-class passengers were crowded onto the shelter deck, taking air before retiring for the night. She scanned in all directions, and finally spotted the girl. She'd shed the coat and was carrying it under her arm as she slipped through the gates that led down to steerage.

19

ABBY

6:30 a.m. Friday, April 12, 1912

Abby woke with her little brother's big toe dangerously close to her left nostril. Under normal circumstances she would have yelped and slapped Felix's grubby foot away, assuming it was one of his pranks. Only these were not normal circumstances . . . not by any means.

Silently shifting away from Felix's feet, Abby listened carefully. She could hear her brother's steady breathing, and Constance's soft snores in the bunk below. That girl slept like a log!

And we're grateful for that, Abby thought.

As quietly as she could, Abby climbed down from the

upper bunk. She switched on a small light—their windowless room was black as pitch without it—and dressed in silence.

Abby stifled a yawn as she brushed out her hair and pinned it neatly up and back. She had barely slept. All night she'd had nightmares about the missing coat, and now she couldn't stop thinking about it. *How could I have been so careless?* she scolded herself. Though she *knew* how . . . the reason was lying behind the curtained bunk with his feet on her pillow!

But the important thing now was to get the coat back before Miss Lucy realized it was gone, which could be soon. Her mistress's daughter was quite sharp, and very observant. When she'd brought her lighter-weight blue coat on deck the day before she'd noted a strange look in the girl's eye. She probably already suspected something was wrong.

I'll tell her I spilled something on it, Abby thought, concocting a confession in her head. It would at least buy her some time to find the thief.

Constance rolled over, yawned and stretched, and sat up. "Good morning!" she chirped. The girl started talking before she even opened her eyes! "I hope you slept well. I slept like a baby! This boat's a big cradle, she is, giving us all a nice little rock-a-bye."

"I slept fine," Abby lied, jumping in before Constance got too far off into a ramble. "Good thing, too. I have so much to do today. How about you? Will you be looking for more eligible officers today?"

"Want to know what I'll be up to, do you?" Constance asked. Abby thought she heard a teasing tone and looked at her questioningly. "Need to know when the cabin will be free . . . for sneaking in boys?" Constance raised her eyebrows.

"I . . . I . . ." she stammered.

"I think perhaps you'd better tell me everything," Constance said, with a smile and knowing nod. The look on her face was the same one Abby's cat would get when she'd cornered a mouse—pleased and ready to pounce. She'd been caught and needed to start talking, fast!

"I didn't have any choice!" Abby blurted. "It was either sneak him aboard or leave him to rot in a workhouse. I'm all he's got since our mother died. And I'm not going back to London . . . there's nothing left for us there. Please don't tell Master Miles! Please don't tell anyone!" Abby felt her throat constricting and tears welling in her eyes.

"Shhhh. Shhhh. Don't fret, my dear!" Constance stood up and placed her hands on Abby's shoulders. "I'm not talking about your little brother," she said calmly. "I've known about him since Cherbourg! I'm talking about that handsome steward I saw you sneaking out of here yesterday!"

Constance smiled and gave Abby a wink. Abby's face flamed hotter than the boilers in the *Titanic*'s belly. "You . . . I . . ."

A light tapping interrupted the conversation before Abby could string together a sentence. Constance wrapped herself in a dressing gown and opened the door a crack to see who was knocking so early. Then she let out a whoop and threw the door open wide.

"Well, speak of the devil!" Constance said, crossing her arms over her chest and stepping back.

Jasper stood in the passage with a tray of scones— enough for three—and a bewildered expression. "Who, me?" he asked.

"Yes, you!" Constance smirked.

"Jasper!" Felix poked his head out of the curtains when he heard the familiar voice, and Abby resisted the urge to shove him back in. He'd obviously heard everything. The cat was out of the bag now—at least with these two.

"Jasper, will you take me to see the bridge today? Please?" Felix begged. His eyes were bright. "I'm going to see every part of this ship before we land!" he hooted. "Maybe we can go up to the crow's nest!"

"We'll see," Jasper said, setting down the tray and rumpling Felix's wild hair.

"We were just talking about you," Constance crowed. "Weren't we, Abby? Of course we were," Constance continued, answering her own question. "Why, do you see how red your sweetheart's face is? That's a dead giveaway."

Jasper turned to Abby. Abby looked at the floor and wished she could sink into it.

"I'm sad to say that you are mistaken," Jasper said to Constance, mercifully taking his eyes off Abby. "Abby is not my sweetheart."

Much to her own amazement, Abby felt her heart drop, but a second later Jasper flashed his crooked smile and added a word that sent her heart right back into her throat . . .

"Yet."

20

LUCY

11:00 a.m. Friday, April 12, 1912

"Isn't it fascinating that we can send messages from the middle of the ocean?" Elisabeth Miles asked, composing a telegram to her brother.

Lucy didn't answer.

Lucy and her mother were seated at a gleaming table in the first-class lounge on A deck, where they had been reading and writing letters and behaving as if last night's episode had never happened. Only Lucy had not written or read more than a few lines. She found herself distracted by the opulence surrounding them. The room was modeled after the Palace of Versailles, with carved English oak, large mirrors, and plush gold and green velvet sofas that made the whole lounge glow.

"Perhaps it's silly to be writing Julian a telegram when we will be together so soon, but everyone has been talking about the Marconi wireless system. It seems a shame not to use it," Elisabeth continued. "I suppose I'll have to find a steward to deliver this to the wireless room." She looked around, searching for a steward, and began to put her writing materials away. "Are you ready to leave?"

Lucy closed her book. Reading was useless. Each time she reached the end of a sentence, she realized she hadn't followed a word of it and had to start over. In addition to the distraction of their surroundings, she could not stop thinking about her coat and the girl she'd seen wearing it. Last night, when she'd finally retired to her bedroom, she'd searched everywhere for her green coat, thinking that her eyes must have been playing tricks on her. The coat was nowhere to be found. But how on earth could it have ended up on someone else? And what was it about the girl wearing it that was so familiar?

"Lucy?" her mother said. "Goodness, where *are* you this morning?"

Lucy tried her best to smile reassuringly. "I'm right here, Mother," she said. "I suppose I'm a bit tired. I didn't sleep well."

"Perhaps you should try one of my dreadful tonics," Elisabeth mused as they made their way out of the lounge and onto the A-deck promenade for some fresh air. "Some of them make me feel as though I will never wake up!"

Lucy bit her lip, feeling guilty for not confessing what was really distracting her. She would not be able to stop thinking about the coat until she knew what had happened to it . . . and that meant getting Abigail alone so she could ask the maid a few questions. She didn't want to bother or worry her mother over something as silly as a coat.

No sooner did she have that thought than Abigail appeared with two overcoats—her mother's camel hair and her own blue one. "Time for a walk?" the maid asked brightly, holding the older woman's coat out so she could put her arms in.

"Perfect timing, O'Rourke. Just give me a moment." Elisabeth smiled and handed off her writing supplies to Lucy. "I'd like to wash up first."

"Of course, Mistress," Abigail replied, lowering the offered coat.

Lucy watched her mother disappear into the lavatory and close the door, then tugged lightly on Abigail's sleeve. "I need a word," she said. Abigail's eyes grew wide in an instant.

"I need you to tell me what has happened to my green coat," Lucy said. "I'm quite certain I saw a girl wearing it last night. In fact I followed her until I saw her heading down to steerage."

Abigail quickly stepped back, as if trying to escape a snare. She was still for a moment, thinking. Then she straightened her shoulders and let out her breath, clearly having made some sort of decision. Lucy hoped she'd decided to tell the truth.

"I'm so sorry, Miss," she said. "I was carrying it with me yesterday morning. I meant to take it back to the stateroom, but I got distracted and laid it over the back of a chair. When I returned to retrieve it, it was gone! It was entirely my fault, and you can take it out of my wages." Abigail spoke faster and faster and her chin dropped. "Just please don't say anything to Master or Mistress Miles!" she pleaded in a quavering voice.

The poor maid looked like a terrified rabbit and Lucy's heart went out to her. She knew she should let the girl off the hook before she died of fright. Besides, she believed what Abigail was telling her. She'd made an absentminded mistake, she was distracted—it was so simple, so logical, and . . .

She felt a corner of her mouth rise. "Distracted by a certain steward, perhaps?" she teased.

Abigail exhaled. She looked a teensy bit more relaxed— and also a bit embarrassed.

"Don't worry. I wouldn't dream of telling Mother *or* Father," Lucy reassured the maid, looking back over her shoulder to make sure her mother hadn't reemerged. She leaned in close. "This is strictly between you and me, and we shall get the coat back before my mother suspects a thing." She tapped her foot on the deck thoughtfully. "We just need to find some reason to slip away so we can go on a search."

"We?" Abigail echoed. "Didn't you say you saw the girl go down to steerage? You don't want to go down there, Miss."

Lucy felt the tingle of anticipation as an idea crept into her head. "Oh, I most certainly do!" she said, looking at the unsent telegram in her hand.

Out of the corner of her eye she saw her mother approach, and stepped forward to speak with her out of Abigail's range of hearing.

"Mother, would you consider letting me deliver the message to Uncle Julian with O'Rourke? I haven't seen the wireless room and I'd really like to get a peek at the Turkish baths as well—I've heard they are magnificent."

Her mother hesitated, so Lucy rushed on.

"O'Rourke works awfully hard, and Father is quite hard on her. Spending a bit of time on a less tedious task might be a welcome relief."

Her mother smiled and reached out a hand to her daughter's cheek. "You are a kind soul, Lucy," she said. "And I suppose I could take some air on my own and meet you at lunch . . ."

Lucy beamed. Her mother didn't often leave her to her own devices, and now she had reason *and* permission to explore more of the ship. It was time for an adventure!

21

ISABELLA

11:25 a.m. Friday, April 12, 1912

Isabella put a hand on her chest, trying to steady her racing heart. She'd successfully made it past the guard at the steerage gates once, but yesterday's guard had been distracted by the man with the scar. There was no such distraction this morning, and even from a distance Isabella could tell that today's guard took his responsibilities *very* seriously. He reminded her of her neighbor's bulldog with his scrunched-up face, underbite, and what appeared to be a permanent scowl. It seemed he never let his body or his gaze leave the exit. Ever.

Slipping back behind a corner, she peeked around, biding her time. Her heart had not slowed the tiniest bit. Getting past the guard was only the first hurdle—she still had to locate her sister and mother. And what about the maid who had seen her in the coat? The young servant obviously knew that the fine green garment was not hers. She'd asked about it as if she recognized it, as if she knew to whom it belonged.

Could it have been hers? she wondered. She stroked the soft wool. Though she doubted the fine coat draped over her arm belonged to a maid, it wasn't completely impossible.

Isabella glanced back at the passage, nibbling her thumbnail. She *must* continue her search! She heard Phillip Miles's gloating laugh in her head and clenched her fists as her impatience grew. She simply had to get past that guard!

Finally another crewmember approached the bulldog-faced man. "Have you heard?" he asked importantly, taking a broad stance and tucking his hands behind his back. "There've been ice warnings."

The first guard raised his chin, and then nodded. "That's not unusual for this time of year," he replied. "Plenty of ice in the North Atlantic in April." He leaned forward and said something else—something Isabella could not hear. The two men kept their heads bent together for several seconds. It was now or never.

Running her free hand over her bodice, Isabella lifted

her head and walked boldly toward the men, easily squeezing between them and the wall, and started up the stairs. She was halfway up the first set of risers and thinking she might have made it unnoticed when a voice boomed out behind her.

"You, there!" one of the guards bellowed. The bulldog, no doubt. "Where do you think you're going? Stop right now!"

Isabella slowed for the briefest of seconds, then made her decision. And ran.

22

ABBY

11:30 a.m. Friday, April 12, 1912

"You're awfully clever, Abigail," Lucy complimented the maid as she followed her from the first-class promenade to the second-class boat deck. They'd delivered the message to the wireless room and were now officially in search of the girl in the green coat. "And you certainly know your way around!"

Abby took a breath. "I suppose I'm learning my way," she answered. Yesterday's frantic search for her brother had taught her a few things, but she could never tell the young Miss Miles where she'd gleaned her knowledge of the boat's layout. Abby was greatly relieved that Lucy wasn't angry about the coat and that she wanted to help locate it in the lower-class areas of the boat, but searching with her employer's daughter posed a significant problem. The decks they needed to search were precisely the places Abby had told her mischievous little brother it was safe to be! And why wouldn't she? There was no possible way she could have known that Miss Lucy Miles might be in those places, too!

If Lucy sees Felix she will certainly recognize him, Abby thought anxiously. *And surely his being on board is too great an offense to keep from her parents.* She nervously fiddled with the bundle of money tied inside her skirts. It was enough to help them once they got to America, but not enough to get them out of jail, or out of the Atlantic Ocean should Master Miles throw them overboard in a fury. *He'd never do that*, she thought . . . *Would he?*

Never mind, she told herself. *All you can do is find the girl and get the coat back as quickly as possible.*

"Do you see her?" Lucy called from behind her. "Anywhere?"

"Not yet, but we will!" Abby replied. She hoped the nervousness in her voice sounded like Lucy's excitement. She led the way off the boat deck and down the main second-class staircase with its oak balustrades and red-and-white linoleum floor. Abby was very familiar with this staircase and rather liked it, or at least appreciated that it went from the boat deck on the very top of the ship all the way down to F deck. They weren't going that far down, however—at least not yet. She stopped on C deck and turned toward the enclosed, glass-windowed promenade, where passengers strolled and children played. She spotted a group of young boys playing with a small ball and quickly scanned their faces to make sure none of them was Felix . . .

"That girl—she was older, and she wouldn't be playing with boys," Lucy said, noticing Abby's fixation on the ballplayers.

Abby swallowed nervously. "Of course not," she agreed. She half hoped that Felix had gone back down to the boilers, though she'd expressly told him *never* to do that again. How quickly things could change! She scanned the deck, not allowing her eyes to linger anywhere for very long.

Lucy had stopped next to a window and was studying the various passengers as they strolled past on the promenade. "Do you suppose the girl would be bold enough to wear the coat again?" she asked. "After all, she knows that she's been seen wearing it. I've been looking for a spot of green all this time, but really I need to remember her face."

Abby hadn't even considered having to find the girl

without the coat! Her eyes instinctually darted to every young girl in sight, hoping to see something familiar. Dark curls and wide-set eyes . . . Were they green? Brown? These were the only features she could remember besides the coat. And no one here fit that description.

"Let's try the library," Abby suggested, trying to stay positive. *That would be a nice place for a girl to spend a bit of time*, she thought, *and it's certainly not somewhere Felix is likely to go.* But as she perused the sycamore-and-mahogany-paneled room and the clusters of passengers visiting or writing letters, she knew at once that the girl they were searching for wasn't there. She wasn't sure how she knew. She could just feel it.

"It's quite a lovely room, isn't it?" Lucy murmured, adding, "It's almost as nice as first class. But I don't see her."

"Me, either," Abby agreed. She had so hoped that they would spot her on the second-class promenade. Swallowing equal parts disappointment and worry, she turned and led Lucy back toward the C deck cabin corridors.

"I only looked into her face for a moment, but somehow I think I'll know her," Lucy suddenly said, pausing slightly outside one of the berths. She spoke very quietly, almost as if she were taking to herself. "I felt like I recognized her even as I was laying eyes on her for the first time." She stopped entirely and looked to Abby. "Does that sound crazy?" she asked, and then went on without waiting for an answer. "There was just something about her face, or the way she wore the coat . . ."

Abby was surprised and pleased that Miss Lucy was talking to her so frankly—as if they were a team, and not a maid and her mistress. "No, it doesn't sound crazy," she said. "And it will no doubt help us identify her."

They made their way through the cabin corridors, seeing no one, and down to D deck to check the second-class dining area and more cabin corridors. But their continued search was fruitless. The girl was nowhere to be found.

Abby sucked in her breath. *At least we haven't spotted Felix, either*, she thought. *Be grateful for that!* And she was. But she was also hard-pressed to face the reality of their situation: They were searching for one girl on the biggest ship in the world, and had nothing but a very basic sense of what she looked like.

She could be anywhere.

23

ISABELLA

11:40 a.m. Friday, April 12, 1912

Isabella lifted her skirts and dashed up the stairwell, taking the steps two at a time.

"I said stop at once!" a voice behind her bellowed. Her legs were burning by the time she reached D deck, and she turned and raced blindly down a second-class cabin corridor. She turned left, then right, then left again. Her breath was heavy and she slowed slightly and glanced back to see if anyone was still following.

"Which way did she go?" a voice called out. A very loud voice. Perhaps more than one!

Panicked, Isabella re-hoisted her skirts and picked up

speed just as a maid came out of a cabin carrying an armful of clean white towels.

"Excuse me!" the maid called, but too late. Isabella careened right into her, upsetting the entire stack of linens.

"I'm so sorry!" Isabella cried, righting herself and glancing momentarily at the jumble of towels on the floor. The maid looked annoyed but didn't say anything as Isabella raced away. She ran past the main second-class dining room and circled back to the stairs, darting past a pair of crewmen. Climbing flight after flight, she found herself at the very top of the ship, the boat deck. She raced over to the rail and pretended to look casually out at the sea while she put on the green coat, steadied herself, and caught her breath. She stood there for several minutes, certain that someone would accost her at any moment.

Breathe, she told herself. *Just breathe.* She breathed, and waited, and nobody came.

When her heart stopped racing and settled into its regular pace, Isabella gave herself another talking to. *All right, then, Isabella. You've made it. It is time to begin your search in earnest.* She was still in an area of the boat reserved for second-class passengers, but on the topmost deck of the ship, and very close to the public first-class areas. That was good.

Isabella reached a hand up to smooth her hair before crossing to the head of the Grand Staircase. Trying to walk like a well-bred young lady, she descended one flight to A deck and made her way to the breathtaking first-class lounge. The room was enormous and modeled after a palace in Versailles—a place Isabella had of course never seen, but she couldn't imagine that it would be any finer than what lay before her. The room was a wonder. Carved English oak with motifs of musical instruments dominated the lounge, along with plush upholstered furniture. The ceiling was high and the room was large and open, but also had cozy alcoves with bay windows overlooking A deck and the blue sea. Just standing inside of it made Isabella feel like she should curtsy to someone . . . or perhaps everyone. She tried not to stare at the women in gorgeous dresses who sat in pairs or small groups, playing cards or relaxing on the velvet sofas with books. The women sat in the palatial room the way Isabella might sit on a park bench—hardly noticing their surroundings. She wondered what it would be like to feel comfortable in such opulence, to fit in. She certainly didn't. She felt like a wart on the nose of a princess!

However out of place *she* felt, it was not hard to imagine the Miles women blending in easily. She could imagine them reading or writing letters on creamy stationary. *Are they here now?* She wanted to believe it was possible, but something in her heart told her it wasn't.

That doesn't mean they won't *be*, she thought. Feeling a tiny spark of hope, Isabella strolled casually over to the small shelf of books provided for passengers and slipped one off the top shelf. She found a settee in one of the alcoves, partially hidden behind a tall fern, and seated herself. From this little spot she would be able to keep both an ear and an eye out, and wait . . .

24

ABBY

2:00 p.m. Friday, April 12, 1912

"Perhaps we can get away later tonight and look some more," Abby said as she and Miss Lucy made their way back to the Mileses' stateroom. They'd continued their search straight through luncheon after making sure Lady Elisabeth had, as suspected, retired to her room.

Abby felt herself relax a bit now that *this* search session had come to an end. She had successfully escaped the horrid possibility of running into her little brother while hunting for the girl in the green coat! For now, at least. And though she would normally be concerned about having left her mistress for so long, the guise of the wireless message errand and the company of her young mistress assuaged her guilt considerably.

"Yes, perhaps," Miss Lucy agreed with a look that was both disappointed and determined. "But we must keep looking. I want to get down into third class . . ."

Her young mistress was not to be deterred, and Abby half wondered if she could lock Felix in their cabin in advance of the proposed steerage search. She'd had no idea that Miss Lucy was so adventurous, or bold—significantly bolder than she would have given her credit for as recently as two days earlier.

It's because she's always so worried about her mother, Abby thought. *She is by her side almost constantly.* Miss Lucy attended her mother much more than Abby did, and she was Elisabeth Miles's maid! Abby was startled to realize that she actually felt a bit sorry for Miss Lucy . . . it couldn't be easy to be so tied to an ailing mother. And it wasn't as if Master Miles was a warm and loving father!

"Thank you for telling me the truth about the coat, Abigail," Miss Lucy said as they approached the Mileses' stateroom, adding, "now let's hope Mother turns in early so we can get out again." Abby could have sworn there was a sparkle in her eye as she said it. It seemed she was actually enjoying this!

"Of course, Miss," Abby said as she twisted the handle and opened the door.

"Mother?" Miss Lucy called softly as they entered. The lights were low and the curtains were drawn, but Abby could make out a motionless shape on the floor. Miss Lucy must have noticed it, too, and she called out again, this time her voice nearly a shriek.

"Mother?" And then, "Abby, turn up the lights!" Elisabeth Miles was slumped on the carpet, her hair unpinned and loose. Miss Lucy shook her arms, trying to awaken her. "Mother?" she cried. "Mother!"

Elisabeth Miles rolled over and groaned. "The tonic . . ." she mumbled. "Your father went to the doctor . . ."

"Help me get her into bed," Miss Lucy said, though Abby was already bending low and helping her mistress to her feet. Together the two girls got the listless woman to her bed and tucked her beneath the covers.

"So tired . . ." she said, her head lolling. "My head . . ." A minute later Lady Miles was entirely asleep.

"Do you think she's all right?" Miss Lucy asked, then went on to answer, "Of course she's not all right. Just look at her!"

Abby could see Miss Lucy's worry dissolving into anger, and the young girl turned abruptly and lunged toward the bottle on the drawing table. She uncorked it and sniffed. Then, her face twisted in frustration, she took a long drink.

"What are you doing?" Abby cried in alarm.

Miss Lucy dropped the bottle to her side. "I've long wondered what's in these tonics," she said, her voice cracking. "What the effects are of the 'medicine' Father forces Mother to take. It's time I see for myself what it does."

Her face shifted again, as if she were smelling something foul. "Mother is right. It tastes terrible," she said.

Then, all at once, she spun around and hurled the entire bottle into the fireplace, shattering it. "Enough!"

"Miss?" Abby asked a bit timidly.

"Oh, Abigail, you don't know. Mother used to be so different, so strong. You saw her yesterday—that was the first time in ages I've seen even a shadow of the way she used to be. She felt good enough to be outside most of the day and still had the energy to go to dinner!" Miss Lucy said, fighting back tears.

Abby nodded. "She was in much better spirits than usual. And she did seem stronger," she agreed.

"Well, she told me yesterday she'd gone off the tonics. She hadn't taken anything," Miss Lucy confided.

"You don't think it's the fresh sea air? Or being on a holiday?" Abby asked. That was what she'd attributed the change to.

"No, she stopped drinking her tonics and was nearly her old self!" Though her voice sounded relaxed, there was an accusation behind Miss Lucy's words—a frightening one. "Do you mind turning down my covers?" she went on, putting her fingers to her forehead. She suddenly sounded extremely tired. "I think I'll turn in. We've had quite a day."

Abby didn't bother to remind her that it was not yet three o'clock in the afternoon. Miss Lucy's words were becoming slurred. Her eyelids drooped as she took a stumbling step toward her bedroom.

If I didn't know better I'd think she was drunk. Or drugged. The thought made Abby's blood freeze for a moment and she shivered, mashing her lips together lest she say something terrible about Miss Lucy's father.

"Of course, Miss." Abby took her arm and guided Miss Lucy to the painted brass bed. The poor girl swayed on her feet as Abby helped her out of her dress and shoes and into her nightclothes. For the second time in twenty minutes,

Abby tucked a Miles woman into bed. Looking down at Miss Lucy's now-peaceful face, she sighed.

Our search for the girl in the coat is concluded for today, she thought, feeling relieved and disappointed at once. Abby cleaned up the glass and sticky tonic mess near the fireplace, careful not to leave a trace for Master Miles to find.

"Good night, Miss Lucy. Good night, Mistress Elisabeth," she whispered before leaving, certain that neither of them heard a word.

25

ABBY

5:30 a.m. Saturday, April 13, 1912

One would think that not having to share her pillow with a pair of twitching feet would have made Abby's night immeasurably more restful. But although the built-in sofa she'd chosen to sleep on instead of sharing the bunk was comfortable, she'd nonetheless spent the entire night tossing and turning. She felt like a tiny dinghy being bandied about by storm waves of worry, washed this way and that with each new surge of fear or concern.

There was the coat to worry about for one—that still needed to be found, and though she had Miss Lucy's assurances she would not tell her parents, as long as the coat and girl were at large there was the chance that Master or

Mistress Miles might see it on the mysterious girl for themselves.

Then there was the worry about the Miles women and the strange medicine Master Miles was forcing upon his wife. Abby wanted to believe that the man was earnest in his attempts to help his wife get well, but seeing Mistress Miles on the floor and then the effect the tonic had on Miss Lucy . . . well, it was clear as day that he was drugging her on purpose. Why?

And then there was her brother. She felt certain Felix was going to be discovered on board at any moment, which would certainly lead to a severe punishment.

But even bigger than these worries was her worry about Felix's future in America, because he depended upon her, and she could depend on, well, nothing.

After fretting away the entire night, it was almost a relief to have to get up and prepare for another day of work. Yawning, she switched on the small lamp and rubbed her eyes. She put on her uniform as quietly as she could and gathered a small parcel containing an everyday shawl and some hairpins for Lucy, in case they had a chance to go looking for the girl in the coat. Constance's snores did not skip a beat and made Abby smile a little as she brushed and pinned her hair.

Before stepping out into the corridor, Abby pushed a corner of the curtain aside and stood on tiptoe to peek in on her little brother. Felix was also sleeping soundly, his lashes dark against his pale face.

He's probably dreaming of seeing the turbines, Abby thought, instantly feeling both amused and frightened. He really was entirely too curious for his own good . . . and for hers! She considered waking him so she could give him a long list of rules to follow before she started her day. Then she had another idea, and let the boy sleep on.

Noiselessly, Abby snuck out of the cabin and eased the door closed.

She had the most efficient route to the Mileses' stateroom memorized now, and aside from a few other servants and stewards the ship's corridors were empty. She stopped outside her employers' door, worried about what she would find given the way she'd left things the day before, and paused to listen.

"I was hoping to run into you!" A now-familiar voice made Abby jump. She whirled, surprised by how pleased she felt to see Jasper's face. His eyes were as warm as ever and she found herself smiling at them, but then when she opened her mouth to speak she faltered. When had it become so difficult to utter words?

"I was hoping to run into you, too," she finally said. Realizing where they were, she led Jasper down the corridor and around a corner. She did not want Master Miles to see her talking to the steward. When they were a safe distance away, she stopped.

"I wanted to ask—"

"I hoped I could—"

They both began to speak at once. Abby stopped and mashed her lips together.

Jasper stopped, too, chuckling. "You first," he said gently.

Abby struggled to untie her tongue again. "I, um, wanted to ask you, officially, if you could help keep an eye on Felix."

"Ha! That's rather funny, because he asked me to do the same for you," Jasper replied.

"He what?" Abby raised an eyebrow. "Since when does—"

Jasper held up his hand and his crooked smile evened out into a grin. "Let me explain. We were talking yesterday, as blokes do, and Felix said you wouldn't be returning to England on the *Titanic*. He said you are planning to stay in New York."

Abby sucked in her breath. This wasn't information to be shared with anyone! "He doesn't know what he's talking about," she said, forcing a laugh and trying to make light of the idea. "He's just a boy with a big imagination . . ."

Jasper put his hand on Abby's shoulder and looked her full in the face.

"Don't worry," he said, his smile completely gone. His face was kind, but serious. "I haven't told any of your secrets, have I? And I have one of my own to share. I'm going to stay on in New York, too." His smile started, the way it always did, on one side of his mouth . . . and grew. "I don't know a soul in America, but since my mum passed over I've got no reason to go back to London. Perhaps you and I can, you know, look out for each other."

Abby's heart fluttered at the thought of knowing another soul in the city where she planned to make a new life. And not just any soul. Jasper.

26

LUCY

11:00 a.m. Saturday, April 13, 1912

Lucy woke up feeling cloudy. What had happened? She shook her head to clear it, trying to recall . . . the search for the girl in the coat . . . the library . . . her mother . . . the tonic! Just the few swallows she'd taken of her mother's "medicine" had sent her straight to bed. How on earth did her mother feel taking multiple doses a day? It was no wonder she was so weak and tired and forgetful!

Lucy fought to control the anger sparking inside her, but did not for an instant regret breaking the bottle and spilling every drop inside. She made her way out to the sitting room and saw the spotless hearth. She was immediately grateful to Abigail for cleaning up the pieces—she was not ready to confront her father. She didn't even want to see him . . . not yet. Fortunately her father seemed none too anxious to spend time with his family, either. He'd already risen and departed without stating his plans.

Lucy's stomach churned and she paced back and forth in the Georgian sitting room, at odds with what to think or do next. She felt caged and queasy, either from the traces of the tonic or the realization that her father was forcing her mother to take something that debilitated her . . . or possibly both.

Does the doctor know what he's up to? she asked herself as she went to check on her mother. Elisabeth had woken briefly but was once again sleeping heavily, and Lucy wondered how much of the tonic she had ingested. She had no idea about either, but Lucy knew she needed to do a bit of digging to learn some things for herself.

Nervous but determined, she took a deep breath and locked the door to their stateroom, then went into her father's bedroom and began to search through his things. She found nothing in his writing desk or his wardrobe. His small leather address book held a myriad of names she had never heard before, but no other notes that seemed suspicious or particularly intriguing. She was about to give up when she decided to check his attaché case one more time.

Buried at the bottom under a bundle of papers she found a small corked bottle with a label that read, "Laudanum." Even through the amber-colored glass she could tell it was empty, but the cork was in place and it was marked with the word *poison* around the small neck. Her heart pounding, she carried it into her room and hid it in the pocket of her blue coat in the wardrobe. She knew that laudanum was a strong drug that was used for pain, and also that it was highly addictive. What was her father doing with his own bottle?

I'll show it to Mother, Lucy thought. She hoped her mother would have a justification, that she would know why her husband had an empty bottle of poison. And she was frightened that she already knew the answer.

Unfortunately, when her mother finally awoke it was immediately clear that she was not alert enough to explain anything. She was tired and groggy, and it took the coaxing of both Abigail and Lucy just to get her out of bed and into a dressing gown. She did not touch her breakfast tray, which by then had grown cold.

To make matters worse, Abigail was not herself, either. She kept glancing at the door, and Lucy had to say everything twice because the distracted girl didn't appear to be listening.

Lucy sighed, feeling both exasperated and trapped. She tried to read, to sketch, to think. Nothing soothed her. Finally she decided she'd had enough. She wanted to get out—she *needed* to.

"Let's go find that coat," she whispered to Abigail, grasping her arm. Abigail bit her lips together nervously and looked back at her with wide eyes, hesitating. "I'll go on my own if I have to," Lucy said, realizing as she said it that she *was* truly bold enough to go on her own—and that even if it was just to distract herself from the questions she had about her father, finding the girl had become strangely important.

"I'll come, Miss," Abigail whispered, her hesitation gone.

With her mother dozing, Lucy let Abigail help her get ready for a trip to steerage. The maid deftly removed the jeweled combs from Lucy's hair and turned her sophisticated coils into a more practical, pulled-back style, securing it with plain pins she pulled from her apron. Next Abigail looked over Lucy's outfit, squinting slightly. Lucy looked down. The gown she wore was nothing special. In fact, Lucy thought it a little out of date. But it did not meet with Abigail's approval and she tiptoed into the bedroom and emerged with a plain, cream-colored dress with an empire waist.

"Lucky I brought this shawl," Abigail said softly when Lucy had the dress on. "It will help hide your dress. We can't have your London style giving us away."

....

Abigail gave a final once-over and nodded her chin sharply before heading for the door. Lucy hurried to keep pace with the maid until they had made it into steerage, where Abigail draped the worn brown shawl around her shoulders and began to move more slowly.

Lucy tried to copy the easygoing posture and air of the third-class passengers as she traipsed behind Abigail. By the time they made it to the stern of the ship and entered the general room on C deck, they weren't catching so much as a sideways glance.

The large, pleasant room had a paneled ceiling and rows of wooden benches. Though it certainly wasn't as finely outfitted as first class, it was nicer than Lucy might have expected, and like everything on the *Titanic*, it was brand-new.

Lucy fiddled with her hair and pulled Abigail's shawl tightly around her to keep the embroidery and pearl buttons on her dress hidden. She so wanted to fit in! The way some of the first-class passengers talked, you'd think third class was filled with rats and filthy beggars. And yet as they wandered and searched the area, Lucy saw mostly families—perfectly respectable-looking families—passing time playing games, talking, or reading.

What she did not see was the girl or the coat.

After nearly an hour Abigail motioned Lucy toward a stairwell. She led her up and out onto the poop deck at the rear of the boat, which served as the third-class promenade. Aside from being downwind of the smoke stacks, the rear deck was quite pleasant and outfitted with comfortable iron and wooden benches. A few spinning air vents dotted about like mushrooms.

Lucy scanned the crowded deck, nearly tripping over a pair of boys playing at her feet. The boys' mother scooped the smallest out of her way and took the other child by the hand, gently scolding her sons to watch what they were doing. Then, before she was even done reprimanding them, she planted kisses on the tops of their heads to soften the blow and released them to continue their play. The brothers ran straight to their father, who crouched down to catch them and eagerly joined in a new game.

Watching the tender exchange, Lucy felt a pang. She looked away, but everywhere her eyes traveled they came across more families laughing and talking, at ease with one another. Seeing them caused an ache she could not explain. She had grown up in the lap of luxury, she had wanted for nothing, and her mother had always been loving. And yet, she suddenly realized, she had never had the comfort and ease of the love that surrounded her now.

It was plain as anything. What Lucy had been hoping for when they boarded the ship—that her father would be somehow transformed and that the three of them could become a caring family of three—was farther away than ever. The realization brought a lump to her throat and she turned toward the far rail. Within moments she'd spotted a welcome distraction.

"Abigail!" she called to the maid who was walking along the row of benches behind her. "Isn't that your steward?"

Abigail looked to where Lucy was gesturing, near the flagpole by the ship rail. Lucy could see why Abigail liked the steward—he was quite handsome, and obviously very friendly. At the moment he was standing beside a boy, and both had their hands to their brows to block the sun as they gazed admiringly up at the ship's massive smokestacks.

Lucy looked back at Abigail expecting to see her smile . . . or flush. But instead of appearing surprised or delighted, Abigail looked decidedly alarmed.

"He can't be of any help!" Abigail said. She rushed to Lucy and took her arm. "I don't think that girl is here, anyway." Abigail was practically pushing Lucy toward the stairs and off the poop deck. "And we've left your mother for too long. We should get back!"

"Shouldn't we just ask him?" Lucy insisted, glancing back at the steward who was now crouching and talking to the passenger. The young boy's face was now visible, and Lucy instantly understood what had rattled Abigail so badly. She turned to the maid with a single eyebrow raised in question. "Or at least go and say hello to your little brother?"

27

ISABELLA

1:00 p.m. Saturday, April 13, 1912

"Let go of me!" Isabella jerked her arm from the clutches of the uniformed steward—the bulldog. She should have known her luck couldn't hold, and silently she cursed herself for her impatience. She'd had to wait over an hour for the Swedish family to leave their berth so she could get ready, and then had stood by the gates for as long as she could stand it, all the while thinking about the fate that awaited her mother and sister if she didn't locate and warn them in time. When the mounting anxiety and desperation grew unbearable, she ran. She surged past the open gates, hoping she could outrun the steward or lose him in the crowd as she'd done the day before. But she had barely gone five paces when she felt an iron grip on her arm.

"You," the steward snorted as he pulled her back roughly. "You're the same girl we saw yesterday." He positioned himself between Isabella and the passage to freedom. With a sneer across his pushed-in face, he looked her up and down in confusion. It was clear to Isabella that he wasn't sure what to make of a girl in such a fine coat coming from E deck . . .

Isabella glanced over the man's shoulder and wondered if she should try to run back the other way, to steerage. Before she could make her decision the steward stepped even closer, nearly pinning her to the wall.

"Are you hard of hearing? I asked where you thought you were going . . ." He cocked his head to look at her out of the corners of his eyes. Isabella did her best to breathe normally. She lifted her chin.

"I'm returning to my suite!" she said in her finest impression of a first-class passenger. Out of the corner of her own eye she spotted a man she thought she'd seen before. It took a moment to place him because he was dressed differently . . . he looked much more like a first-class passenger than the last time she'd laid eyes on him. But she was certain he was the man who had been trying to get out of steerage two days ago. Isabella shuddered at the sight of his scar, and the realization that he was watching them with interest.

"My *first-class* suite!" Isabella said, refocusing on the steward.

Her acting may not have been the best, but it was enough to make the bulldog step back. He looked confused for a second time, and then his expression changed. "Oh, I see," he smirked, raising his thick eyebrows. "I'm asking the wrong question. Where have you *been*, Miss? What exactly have you been getting up to in third class?"

Isabella tried to look haughty and offended. She pursed her lips and breathed through her nose. "I don't see how that is any of your concern," she replied, narrowing her eyes.

"Right." He nodded, though he clearly did not believe her. "I'll need to see your ticket, of course."

Of course. Isabella wished she could slap the smug look off the steward's squinched-up face, but she had no choice but to continue the ruse. "I do not carry my ticket for passage with me," she replied with mock disdain.

The steward smiled coldly. "Then we will just check the passenger list." He grasped Isabella's arm a little more firmly than was necessary and led her to a nearby supply area. "Your name?" he asked when he had located the list.

"Miles," Isabella replied. It wasn't a lie. Not really.

The man with the scar turned in her direction.

"Hmmph." The steward ran a thick finger down the manifest, stopping when he found what he was looking for. "Hmph," he snorted. "Here you are." He looked momentarily defeated, and Isabella thought he might let her go. Then his sneer was back. "Let's just go have a word with your father," he said, pulling her along with him toward B deck. "I have a feeling Mr. Miles will have something to say about you mixing with the vermin in steerage."

28

ABBY

1:00 p.m. Saturday, April 13, 1912

Felix!

Abby could not breathe. She could not speak. Miss Lucy had spotted Felix, and the game was up! If only it *were* a game and not their futures at stake!

"I . . . I . . ." Abby stammered, struggling to find the words to explain to Miss Lucy what her brother was doing aboard the *Titanic*. For a split second she considered denying it, telling her mistress that the boy talking to Jasper wasn't her brother. But aside from their obvious resemblance and the fact that Miss Lucy had seen him on numerous other occasions, she had been nothing but good to her—right down to her willingness to venture into steerage to help Abby find the expensive coat she'd so carelessly lost! Miss Lucy deserved the truth. And besides, Abby was exhausted from trying to keep Felix hidden and living in constant fear of being caught in her own web of lies.

"Miss Lucy, I had to . . ." Lucy held up a hand, silencing her. Abby met her gaze and was surprised to see that the look on her employer's face was not anger or even shock . . . it was admiration!

"How did you do it?" Lucy asked. There was a sparkle in her eyes that had not been there this morning. "How did you manage to get him aboard?"

Abby glanced around. Her mouth was bone dry.

"Don't worry," Lucy said, dropping her voice to a whisper. "I won't say a word. To be perfectly honest I'm relieved to see Felix. I . . . I was afraid to ask what kind of arrangements you'd made for him while we are away from London."

"Your father wanted him to go to a workhouse." Abby's eyes welled with tears. "But I just couldn't! I was desperate. I put him inside a steamer trunk and . . ."

Lucy blinked back tears of her own—she was laughing and crying at once. "Oh, you didn't!" she gasped. "You put him in a trunk? That's brilliant."

Abby couldn't help but smile back. "I had to. I need us both to land in America . . . I . . . I'm planning to stay there."

"Oh, Abigail." Her eyes alight, Lucy put a hand on Abby's arm. "How unbelievably brave you are!"

"Or foolish," Abby added.

"Honestly, I'm not sure I would be so capable if I were the one to lose my mother and—"

This time it was Abby who held up a hand. She didn't feel able to continue the conversation. The emotions she worked so hard to contain were threatening to break the surface of her composure. It was all too much! She did not want to become hysterical here, now, in front of Lucy, Jasper . . . and especially Felix.

Abby kept her back to the boys and Lucy thankfully did not push further. She kept her hand on Abby's arm, steadying her, and spoke softly. "The way you manage to care for so many others without a soul to care for you is a wonder, Abigail. Your mother would be very proud. I know she would."

Abby drew a ragged breath. She swallowed hard and managed a small smile. "Thank you, Miss," she murmured. Though they brought a wave of emotions to the surface,

Lucy's words meant more to her than she could know, and Abby was grateful for the kindness.

"So what do you say? Shall we enlist those two young sailors to help find my coat?" Lucy asked, lightening the mood and giving Abby another reason to be in her debt. She tilted her head back toward the spot where Jasper and Felix had been standing, but when Abby turned her gaze to the rail there was no one there.

Jasper and Felix had disappeared.

29

ISABELLA

1:30 p.m. Saturday, April 13, 1912

Isabella nearly laughed to herself as the confused steward tried to find the way to the first-class staterooms. Instead she hid her smile and silently let him steer her up and down various corridors and staircases, leading them in circles for a good forty-five minutes.

"Ridiculous ship," he grumbled, tugging on her arm. Finally he seemed to recognize where they were. Prodding her up a flight of stairs, he pushed her toward the elevators near the Grand Staircase. Though he didn't seem convinced that she was indeed a first-class passenger, the possibility that she could be seemed enough to keep him from handling her too roughly.

They rode in silence. With the elevator's accordion doors locked tight, there was no point in trying to get away. Isabella knew she was trapped and would soon be standing before her biological father.

I'll have to face him sometime, she thought, though she had hoped to contact her mother and sister before coming face-to-face with Phillip Miles. As she stepped off the elevator, she felt more like a convict being sent before a judge than the daughter of a first-class passenger. Had her whole plan been doomed from the start? Who was she to be counting on a mother and a sister she'd never met? The Miles women were strangers to her, and she to them.

The steward gave a sharp rap on the Mileses' stateroom door without releasing the firm grip on Isabella's elbow. Several long seconds passed, and hope flickered in Isabella's chest. If Mr. Miles was not in his room, he would be extremely difficult for the steward to find—particularly since he obviously knew little about the ship's layout. It would only buy her time, but time was better than nothing!

Isabella heard footsteps approaching on the other side of the door and her heart pounded. The latch turned and Phillip Miles opened the door, his dark brows lowered in a scowl. He looked them both up and down. "Yes? What is it?"

"May we have a word, sir?" The steward still had the smug look on his face, and now made a move toward the door. Instead of asking them in, however, Miles glanced backward, stepped into the corridor, and quickly closed the door behind him.

"My wife is resting. She's very frail," he announced. "We'll have to talk somewhere else."

Isabella craned her neck to get a glimpse of Mrs. Miles— the stranger who was, in fact, her mother—before the door shut, but saw nothing.

Miles glared at her. He glared at the steward, who looked slightly less arrogant under Miles's harsh gaze, and then turned and walked briskly toward the open decks.

The steward hurried Isabella along behind Miles. She was finding it increasingly difficult to breathe and her legs felt like they had leaden weights tied to them. It was as if Miles had already tossed her overboard and she was sinking under the waves.

Finally, Phillip Miles stopped in a more or less empty area of the promenade deck and turned to wait for them to catch up.

"Now. What is this about?" he asked gruffly.

The steward stood taller and puffed out his chest. "Your

daughter was down in steerage, sir," he reported, his lip curling. "I caught her in the bowels of the ship myself. Now it isn't my place to—"

"My daughter?" Phillip Miles interrupted. "Where is she?" He glanced past the steward, past Isabella, looking for Lucy Miles.

Isabella swallowed hard and squared her shoulders. She took a gasping breath. "I'm right here, Father," she said boldly. "I'm afraid it wasn't as easy to get rid of me as you thought."

30

LUCY

2:00 p.m. Saturday, April 13, 1912

Lucy stopped short at the top of the stairs. The sound of her father's voice sent a shiver down her spine. He was on the promenade deck, speaking to someone in a harsh tone. She thought she heard the word "daughter" and hoped against hope she was mistaken. She and Abigail had been away for quite a long time, and it was entirely possible that he was looking for her. Although she doubted he was actually concerned—it was far more likely that he was upset with her for leaving her mother.

Lucy looked back at Abigail, putting a finger to her lips and motioning for her to come closer. The two inched toward the doorway at the top of the stairs. Lucy wanted to see the person her father was talking to, or rather shouting at. His voice had already risen considerably, and he sounded angry.

"But I paid the doctor to . . ." He halted, as if he'd just realized that he was saying too much. "That's preposterous!"

Lucy peeked around the edge of the door and instantly spotted another figure—a man she was certain she'd seen before but now could not place—before her eyes found her father.

His back was toward the stairwell, but there was no mistaking him. "You're nothing but a grubby little urchin trying to get your hands on my money!" he snarled.

By taking a small step forward, Lucy was able to see whom he was yelling at. She reached back and squeezed Abigail's hand to keep from crying out. It was the girl in the green coat!

Abigail squeezed back to let her know that she saw her, too, and they both watched, transfixed, as the girl pulled an envelope out of the coat pocket.

"I am your daughter. I have proof," she said. Her voice trembled as much as her hand as she held the envelope toward Lucy's father. He snatched it, turning away from the girl and the steward holding her elbow before pulling a few weathered pages from the envelope.

Lucy stepped back so her father wouldn't see her if he looked up, but there was no need. His attention was entirely focused on the documents. His face contorted as his eyes darted back and forth. Lucy felt herself holding her breath. She had seen her father's temper more times than she could count, and knew all too well when he was about to fly into a rage.

"This is nonsense!" he bellowed. He stared daggers at the girl and took two slow steps toward her. Lucy was mesmerized by the girl's look of fear as her father held the papers close to her face. Her stomach dropped. She knew exactly what it was like to be on the receiving end of her father's wrath. He pushed the papers closer to the girl's face. Then he pulled them back and held them over the water instead, taunting her for a moment before ripping them to shreds and letting the pieces fall into the sea.

"No!" the girl shrieked, breaking from the steward's grasp and frantically reaching over the rails as if she could catch the scraps fluttering down to the ocean. "No!"

"You have nothing!" Lucy's father snarled. The girl turned back to him. Her cheeks were wet, and as the reality of his words sunk in, her face crumpled completely.

"Nothing," Lucy's father repeated before looking to the

steward. "This gutter rat is no daughter of mine. Take her back to steerage where she belongs before I have you fired for falling for such a ridiculous ruse."

Lucy felt Abigail's hand still gripping hers, and they watched in horror as the steward yanked the girl in the coat toward their hiding place.

"You don't understand," the girl said, pleading with him and trying to pry his hand off her arm.

"I understand that you won't ever make a fool of me again!" the steward hissed, pulling her ever closer to Lucy and Abigail.

Lucy was frozen in place, but felt Abigail pull her out of the steward's path. She watched, transfixed, as the large man dragged the girl down the stairs. The scene felt like it wasn't real. Like it *couldn't* be real. Lucy was still staring after them, when the girl suddenly stopped pulling at the steward and turned to look up at her, as if Lucy had called her name. She hadn't, of course. She hadn't even the slightest idea what her name might be!

Lucy locked eyes with the girl and the world slowed. She had the same feeling of recognition she'd had the first time she'd set eyes on her, and it sent a shiver up her spine. The girl's mouth opened, filled with an unspoken . . .

something. They continued to stare at each other as the girl was dragged away, and Lucy knew deep inside that she was not the only one who saw it. They each recognized something in the other—the familiar way she held her mouth, the shape of her eyes, the slight turn of her nose. They both understood that something had been taken from them, and against all odds they had just found it.

"She's telling the truth," Lucy said in a whisper when she couldn't see the girl any longer.

Abigail looked confused.

"That girl is my father's daughter," Lucy said more loudly. "That girl is my sister!"

31

ABBY

2:15 p.m. Saturday, April 14, 1912

Abby took Lucy firmly by the arm to help keep her upright. Every bit of color was gone from her young mistress's face, and if she hadn't been holding the rail, Abby was certain Lucy would have fallen headlong down the stairs after the girl in the green coat—the girl Lucy believed to be her sister.

Abby had dozens of questions, but her doubts about the coat thief's outrageous claim—that Phillip Miles was her father—had diminished the moment Lucy told her it was true. Besides, this was not the moment to ponder the hows or the whys.

The girl's desperate protests continued to echo up the stairwell, answered only by the steward's angry grunts. Abby kept hold of Lucy's arm while Lucy pulled her down the stairs after them. For a long moment neither of them spoke; then Lucy broke the silence, muttering softly. Abby wasn't sure if she was talking to her, or to herself.

"I know her. I feel I know her. She must be my father's daughter, but we've never . . . I . . ." She trailed off, then turned back to Abby. "I have to help her!"

Abby nodded without slowing down. Yes, they had to help her, but how? Her thoughts flew as fast as her feet, and Abby was so focused on keeping herself and her companion upright that she nearly ran into someone coming up the stairs.

"Jasper!" Abby stopped short and pulled Lucy to a stop beside her. The always-smiling steward wasn't smiling. Abby anxiously looked over his shoulder, but her brother was not there.

"Where's Felix?" she blurted.

Jasper looked from Abby to Lucy, his eyes uncertain.

"It's okay," Abby assured him, understanding the unspoken question. "She knows." She squeezed Lucy's arm tighter—again grateful for her discretion and kindness in agreeing to keep Felix a secret.

"He slipped away from me. We were on the poop deck and I was telling him about the smokestacks and . . . he just disappeared. I was hoping he was with you," Jasper confessed. "I'm so sorry. I was trying to keep him occupied—"

A loud wail echoed up the stairwell and Lucy gasped.

Abby sucked in a quick breath. "Felix will be fine," she told Jasper. She wished she had time to explain everything. She wished she *understood* everything. "But right now we need to talk to that girl." She pointed down the stairs and realized that Jasper must have passed her on the way up. "She has Miss Lucy's coat, and that steward is taking her back to steerage."

"Please, we have to help her!" Lucy added, stricken. She started to pull away from Abby to go after the girl on her own.

Jasper put a hand on Abby's arm. "No," he said firmly. "I'll go. You two wait here."

Abby watched Jasper turn and race down the stairs, taking them two at time. Lucy started to follow, but Abby held her back. "I think we should do as he says—he'll have better luck without us."

Lucy looked down. It was true—a girl, even one traveling in first class, didn't stand a chance of convincing a crewman of much of anything. Jasper was young, but he had his uniform. "Even if he can't bring her back, he can find out where she's being taken."

Lucy nodded, but Abby could tell that dark worries were already gnawing at her companion. She tried to think of something to say to ease Lucy's concerns, but was too distracted by the pit of worry growing in her own stomach. Despite what she'd told Jasper, she *was* upset that Felix was on his own . . . upset and worried. Why did her little brother always pick the absolute worst times to go missing?

"He'll be all right," Lucy said, reading Abby's troubled thoughts. "You said yourself that he's a scrapper."

Abby rolled her eyes and forced a smile. "That he is," she admitted.

The girls' conversation ended abruptly when they heard someone approaching from below. Abby held her breath and strained to make out the details. There were the footfalls of more than one person . . . and was that a male voice?

When Jasper came around the corner leading the girl in the coat, Abby could scarcely believe her eyes. The girl looked petrified, while Jasper looked as though he'd caught a prize fish. He flashed his crooked smile and Abby returned it.

Lucy stepped toward the girl without hesitation. She reached out her hand. "I'm Lucy Miles," she said, introducing herself properly, as if they weren't both wearing clothes that begged explanations, as if they hadn't been secretly stalking each other. "And you must be . . . my sister?"

Abby stepped closer to Jasper. "How did you do that?" she asked him in a whisper. "How did you get her away from that other steward?"

"Oh, you're not the only one around here who's pulled a fast one or two," Jasper whispered back. He looked from Abby to the sisters on the stairs and back. Clearly everyone in the stairwell had some tricks up their sleeves. "Speaking of scalawags, I'd better get back to tracking down that brother of yours before he gets into trouble. You can explain all of this to me later."

Abby watched Jasper leave, wondering if she'd ever be able to explain "all of this." She wanted to go with Jasper and find Felix . . . she needed to see her brother, to know that he was all right. And also to pinch his cheeks for running off!

Then she looked at Lucy, who was holding the hand of her newfound sister. The air was charged with questions and unspoken truths, and as much as she wanted to go, it was clear that she needed to stay for Lucy's sake.

32

ISABELLA

2:30 p.m. Saturday, April 13, 1912

Isabella struggled to catch her breath. She was relieved to be away from the bulldog steward, but still felt as if she were blindfolded and walking a tightrope. Each step was an act of faith . . . she had no idea what lay below. If she slipped, would she plummet several stories to her death, or drop onto a feather bed?

She looked down at her hand, still clutching the fingers of the girl who had introduced herself as Lucy Miles, then turned her gaze toward Lucy's face. She could see the resemblance to her father—their father—but, thank goodness, none of the cruelty. A small noise escaped her throat. A strangled sob of relief, she realized. But was it premature?

"Come," Lucy said, tugging Isabella up the stairs and into the open air. Out on deck it was easier to breathe, but harder to hold back tears. Isabella found she could not contain her emotions any longer. Her shoulders shook and she covered her face. After everything she'd been through, this was too much.

"Oh, don't cry!" Lucy said. "It's going to be all right." Isabella felt Lucy put an arm around her shoulders and slowly raised her head to look at the older girl . . . her sister . . . again. Her expression was kind. Isabella glanced over at the maid who had followed them up the stairs and was studying her carefully. Her expression was not so kind.

"What are you doing with Miss Miles's coat?" the maid demanded suddenly.

"Don't traumatize her, Abigail!" Lucy scolded, though not harshly. "We have plenty of time to unravel everything." She smiled gently at Isabella and added, "I think you might hold the answers to many mysteries." Lucy eyes were full of something Isabella couldn't quite identify. Excitement? Hope? She wiped her cheeks with the back of her hand and tried to catch her breath.

"Let's start with who you are," Lucy said.

Isabella swallowed hard. Who was she, exactly? It was a

simple question, one that she could have answered easily up until a few days ago. Oh, how things had changed!

"My name is Isabella," she said slowly. "And I'm so sorry I took your coat! I was looking for you . . . and I found it on deck. I didn't know it was yours, and certainly didn't mean to steal it!" She unbuttoned the fine wool garment and was about to shrug out of it when Lucy stopped her again.

"You were looking for *me*?" she asked, her surprise obvious. "Why?"

"I wasn't looking for you exactly . . . not at first." Isabella leaned back against the deck rail, unsure of where to begin. It was all so complicated!

"Perhaps we should sit," Lucy said. She led them to some deck chairs in a quiet corner. When they were seated, she looked at Isabella with eyes so nearly like the pair that stared back at her from the glass each day that Isabella had to look away.

"Can we start at the beginning?" Lucy asked. "Please tell me who you are and why you were looking for me."

Isabella looked from Lucy, to the maid, and back. It all felt entirely surreal! And yet here she was, on board the *Titanic*, sitting across from a sister she'd never known. The thing to do now, it seemed, was to simply tell the truth.

"Miss, I am your sister," Isabella said. The words felt strange in her mouth, and sounded even stranger in the air. She expected Lucy to laugh or gasp or slap her. The wealthy young girl had no reason to believe her, and any proof that Isabella might have been able to provide was now somewhere in the icy North Atlantic. She had nothing to offer . . . and nothing to lose. She drew a deep breath. "My name is Isabella."

Lucy stared intently for several more long seconds. "You *are* my little sister, aren't you?" she asked. Her voice wavered and her hand flew up to cover her mouth. "You don't have to say it again. I *know* you are! I recognized you the moment I saw you." Her eyes glistened as she threw both of her arms around Isabella.

Isabella was too stunned to hug her sister back. She felt relief—Lucy believed her! But she still felt afraid.

She pulled away. She had more to tell, and much of it would be difficult to hear.

"My parents, the parents who raised me, bought me a ticket and put me aboard. They gave me a letter that explained who I was and why I was to travel to America on the *Titanic*."

"And Father threw it away," Lucy finished for her.

Isabella nodded. "There was also a birth certificate," she explained. "It was supposed to have been destroyed, but one of your servants pulled it from the fireplace and recently delivered it to the parents who raised me. It was my only proof that I am part of the Miles family, and my adoptive parents hoped it would compel your father to help me when we reached New York. That is why I was looking for him.

"When I found the coat I thought it would help me go unnoticed during my search of the first- and second-class areas of the ship. I put it on so I could look for all of you," she confessed. "I never meant to steal it."

Lucy and the maid exchanged a look, and her sister touched the worn shawl she was wearing. "And I wore this to search for you," she said.

Isabella would have liked to smile at the coincidence—the two of them trading places to look for each other—but she had not yet told Lucy the most difficult part of her story. "Wearing your coat allowed me to find your . . . our . . . father," she hesitated, searching for the courage needed to get the next part out. "Only when I did, I wished I hadn't." A fresh wash of tears sprang to Isabella's eyes at the memory of Phillip Miles boasting about his evil scheme. His plan was so cruel it was difficult for her to speak it out loud, and yet she had no choice.

"I overheard him bragging about putting your . . . I mean our . . . mother in a sanatorium in America, and sending you to boarding school! He means to go back to England with your mother's money and leave your uncle to foot the bill. When I heard that, I knew I had to find you, to warn you."

Lucy drew back from Isabella. Her eyes narrowed and she wiped away the tears that had been threatening to spill from them. "Father." She spoke the word under her breath, as if it was something that should not be uttered out loud. "I've had misgivings about him for some time now . . . But this . . ." The dismay on Lucy's face hardened into anger. "I never would have predicted something so nefarious!"

"Nefarious indeed," a deep voice said.

Lucy looked up and blanched. A man was looming over them . . . a man with an angry red scar running down his cheek.

33

LUCY

3:30 p.m. Saturday, April 13, 1912

Lucy watched Abby shrink back in fear, but her little sister didn't seem intimidated in the least.

"You!" Isabella said.

The man's face softened as he gazed down at the three girls. "Name's Greer," he said. "Nicholas Greer. Are you Phillip Miles's daughter?" he asked Lucy.

"Daughters," Lucy corrected, glancing at her sister with a small smile. "Yes."

"And your mother, Elisabeth Miles, is she traveling with you?"

"Would you mind telling me why that is any of your concern?" Abby blurted protectively.

The man shuffled his feet on the deck, seeming suddenly uncomfortable in his clothes. "Your father owes people a lot of money back in London, Miss. I was paid to follow him, to make sure he settles his debts. But I didn't know about his family when I accepted the job . . ."

Greer trailed off. His face was full of apology, and Lucy saw that up close his scar was far less noticeable beside his warm eyes.

"I'm supposed to see to it that your father settles his accounts no matter what. But when I got wind of his plans . . . I . . ."

He trailed off a second time, as if he wasn't sure he should continue. He looked out to sea for a moment before turning back to the girls and clearing his throat. He had made a decision.

"Miss Miles, you tell your mother not to let her husband lay hands on any more of her money. He has done enough."

Lucy stared up at Greer. How strange that he knew more about her father than she did. And stranger still that the story she'd just heard from her sister was now confirmed by this rough-looking man she'd only just met.

This kind, *rough-looking man*, she corrected herself.

Lucy reached out a hand and touched the edge of his sleeve. "Thank you, Mr. Greer," she said. "I will warn my mother just as you suggest."

Nicholas Greer smiled faintly and gave a small nod. He looked satisfied and also resigned. He had failed to do his job the moment he warned the girls.

Greer tipped his hat. "Well, good afternoon, then," he said.

Lucy watched him go, surprised to realize that her father's awfulness had quite plainly brought out the good in Nicholas Greer.

34

ABBY

4:00 p.m. Saturday, April 13, 1912

Abby watched Nicholas Greer walk stoically across the deck, suddenly realizing that his eyes reminded her of her late father's. Her heart was heavy with the thought. Oh, how she missed her parents!

"I have seen him several times," Isabella told Lucy. "At first trying to get out of steerage and later on deck," she squeezed her sister's hand. "But I had no idea he was looking for you!"

"I also saw him but did not know," Abby agreed, feeling at once a part of this conversation and also removed from it—from the two girls sitting across from her. She'd been listening rapt to Isabella's tale, sometimes even feeling as though Isabella was a gift to her as well. And yet something inside told her that this was not true. Something reminded her that she was separate from the Miles sisters . . . maybe even more separate now that there were two of them.

Could she truly be Miss Lucy's sister? Abby wondered. It seemed she must be, for who could come up with such an outrageous tale? Besides, Isabella's resemblance to Miss Lucy was undeniable. That seemed proof enough. And Miss Lucy had said she could feel their sisterhood.

But there was something else. One piece of the puzzle was stuck in the back of her mind and quickly growing into a question—a question she could barely form into words. A question that needed to be asked immediately.

"Pardon me, Miss Isabella," she interrupted, her stomach suddenly in knots. "How did you happen to come by that birth certificate? Who gave it to your mother?"

Isabella turned, her brow creasing in thought. "Mother wrote in her letter that she got it from a maid . . . a maid in the Miles house," she replied.

Lucy's hand flew to her mouth while tears sprang to Abby's eyes.

"Oh, Abigail, it could only have been your mother!"

Abby knew it was true before Lucy said it, and it unleashed a terrible thought that sent her mind reeling. She felt as though the entire ship suddenly listed and her whole world was thrown off-balance.

"Do you think . . . do you think that's wh—" Abby could not get the words out.

Isabella stared at her, wide-eyed and not quite comprehending. "Your mother brought the letter," she repeated.

"And now my mother is dead," Abby said.

A heavy silence fell over the girls.

"She couldn't live with Master Miles's wrong, so she made a choice," Abby blurted as she swallowed her tears. Isabella was here because of her mother's bravery and conviction. "A choice that cost her everything."

"Oh, Abigail!" Lucy rushed to put her arms around Abby as the weight of the sacrifice and the horror of what her father had done crushed down upon them both.

"My mother gave her life," Abby said in a whisper.

Lucy leaned in close and spoke so softly that Abby could barely hear. "And my father took it."

Abby laid her head on Lucy's shoulder and let the tears fall. She sat there for several long moments, until she felt the other girl's back go rigid. Until Lucy pulled away slightly. She was looking at Abby with fire in her eyes.

"We won't let him get away with it," she vowed.

35

LUCY

10:45 p.m. Sunday, April 14, 1912

"Whatever is the matter, Lucy?" Elisabeth Miles asked, looking up from the book in her lap. Lucy turned on her heel and paced across the room, eyeing the clock on the mantel. This had been the absolute longest day of her life, and she was exhausted. Her mother, on the other hand, seemed full of energy after her lengthy tonic-induced sleep. She'd slept for a night and most of a day and, after another night's sleep, was now perky as a chipmunk when she would normally be fast asleep. It was fortuitous in a way, since Abigail and Isabella were going to appear at the door any moment, but Lucy was drained and anxious.

"I'm just restless, I suppose," Lucy replied, wondering if she should be easing her mother into the shocking news she was about to receive. Was there a way to soften the blow? It didn't seem possible.

Lucy was so incredibly angry with her father! She had successfully avoided him all day except for dinner, and had then shoved food into her mouth to prevent herself from confronting him.

All three girls agreed it would be best to talk to Elisabeth Miles together and had concocted the plan to meet in the stateroom while Phillip indulged in his post-dinner card game. Dinner had been torturous, but now here she was, pacing in their sitting room and waiting for Abigail and Isabella—her sister.

Her sister! Lucy looked at her mother's calm face. How would she react when she heard she had another living daughter? Would she believe Isabella was hers? Had she ever wondered whether her baby was alive? Had her father told her mother that the baby had died? Lucy felt certain Isabella was telling the truth, that she belonged to them. She could feel their sisterhood in her bones. Would her mother feel the connection, too?

Lucy turned on her heel for the fifteenth time and stole another look at the clock. *What on earth could be keeping them?* she wondered. The longer she had to wait, the more apprehensive she became. In addition to everything else, there was the very real concern that this new information would be more than her mother could bear. Even though she had once been a strong woman, her husband's constant undermining had taken a toll—he had been poisoning her with words and with potions for a long time.

"Lucy, please sit down. You're making me anxious," her mother said.

But Lucy did not sit down, for she had just remembered the empty bottle of laudanum. She strode to the wardrobe and pulled it out.

"Mother, I found this in Father's attaché. Do you know why he would have it?"

Elisabeth Miles looked from Lucy's face to the bottle, and back to her daughter's face. Lucy momentarily wondered if she would be scolded for searching through her father's things, but her mother's anger was not directed at her.

"I can think of several reasons, all of them unfortunate," she replied darkly. Lucy had the sense that her mother had had enough, and worried anew that the surprises were only beginning. She sat down and drew a long breath. She could not keep the news of Isabella in a moment longer! "Mother, there's something I need to—"

There was a knock on the door, and Abigail came into the room.

Elisabeth tilted her head, perplexed, and then realized that the maid was not alone. Isabella, white as a freshly washed sheet, stepped into the room behind her. The dark-haired girl's eyes were glued to the fine new carpet on the floor.

"And who is this young . . ." Elisabeth trailed off. She looked from her maid, to Lucy, to the girl standing before her, and back to Lucy. Her jaw dropped, and the book she'd been holding fell to the floor as her hands began to tremble.

Lucy set a hand on her mother's knee. "Mother," she said. "This is Isabella. She is—"

A gut-wrenching sob burst from Elisabeth's throat, halting Lucy's explanation. Lucy felt a moment of panic. Was her mother all right? Oh, she never should have done this!

"Isabella," Lucy's mother repeated, letting the name linger in the air while she got to her feet. "Our Isabella!" She opened her arms and Isabella rushed into them.

"I knew you were alive," Elisabeth whispered into Isabella's hair. "I simply knew it . . . all these years. My daughter. My baby." She pulled back to look at Isabella at arm's length. "But what has happened to you?" She turned to pull Lucy into the embrace, and tears ran down their cheeks as they clung to one another—the three of them together for the very first time. Finally, Lucy pulled back and took a breath.

"Perhaps you should sit down again, Mother. Though this is a happy moment for us, it is not a happy story."

Her mother did not sit—she stood taller. "I am aware of that, Lucy. I am a part of this story, and I have suspected for some time that things are not as they have seemed . . . not as they should have been. This proves it.

"Come, all three of you. Let us sit and tell one another everything we know." They pulled a few chairs around the sitting room table and sat down.

"Go ahead," Lucy said, nodding at her sister encouragingly.

Isabella took a breath and began to tell her story. "I had no idea I was adopted until I was on board the *Titanic*. Mother—my adoptive mother, Ruth James—gave me a letter." Isabella's voice caught. "The parents who raised me are poor but they did all they could for me. They are kind,

hardworking people. And they love me, I'm certain of that."
She paused, her eyes welling. Lucy squeezed her sister's
hand. The poor girl had been through so much—including
being torn away from the only parents she had ever known.
She must have been missing them terribly!

"I have been very lucky," Isabella choked out.

Elisabeth leaned forward and touched Isabella's cheek.
"Yes, being well loved and looked after is lucky indeed.
I, for one, am grateful to them for caring for you."

Lucy's heart swelled as she looked at her mother and
sister together. Then she felt the glow of happiness recede at
the thought of her father. Not only did he not love her, he
was out-and-out evil. "Isabella, tell Mother what you learned
when you were searching for Father," she said gravely.

Isabella's eyes grew wide with worry. "It's all right,"
Lucy reassured her. "She already suspects, and now she needs
to know."

"I overheard him talking. He was telling another man
that he plans to have you admitted to a sanatorium in America,
and Lucy enrolled in boarding school. I heard him boasting
that he could get your brother to pay for it all. He wants to
leave you both and return to England with as much of your
family's fortune as he can take . . ."

Lucy saw her mother's spine stiffen even as her jaw dropped open in shock. "Does he now?" she said in almost a whisper. "Because I imagine he's already run through my share of the family fortune." Her eyes narrowed in anger, but behind her fury was something else—something steadfast. "Oh, Phillip. I'm afraid you are in for a few surprises . . ."

A tiny smile played on Elisabeth's lips and Lucy felt her heart leap in her chest. Her mother was not weak—she was strong. And smart. Despite her father's attempts to manipulate her mind and health, Elisabeth Miles was still her very capable self.

"Mother, what happened?" Lucy asked. "How did Isabella come to be adopted if we all lived in London?"

Elisabeth stroked Isabella's hair. "I remember the night you were born as if it were just yesterday. You decided you were ready to come into the world much earlier than we expected, and there you were, tiny as a kitten and shouting your little head off. Your father wasn't at the birth, but I remember hearing his voice soon after you appeared. I'd only had you in my arms for a moment when the doctor took you from me so that your father could have a peek. I heard you hollering at him the hallway."

Lucy saw a faraway look come into her mother's eyes.

"The doctor came back without you. I asked for you, but he gave me something to drink and told me to rest. When I awoke the house was quiet. The doctor told me you had died—that you were too small to survive. I didn't believe it. I'd seen your strength. I'd felt it. But I was so ill in those next days I was in a stupor. When I finally came out of it, I had to accept that I had lost you . . ."

Tears streamed down Elisabeth's face as she gazed at Isabella, and hazy memories began to swirl in Lucy's mind. She remembered a baby crying. She remembered the bustle and anticipation, and later the dark quiet. She remembered the shadow of sadness.

"That man," Elisabeth said, her teeth gritted tightly together. "That wretched man told me you were dead."

"I suspect he paid the doctor to tell you that," Isabella said. "And he tried to burn the birth certificate as well."

"What's this? Another letter?" Elisabeth asked.

Lucy let out her breath and reached for Abigail's hand. "Mother, that's how Isabella's adoptive parents found out. They got a letter from a maid. Our maid."

"I suspect my mother couldn't live with the awful lie, Mistress," Abigail said.

Lucy watched as a look of true horror crossed her mother's

face. "Oh no," she gasped. "Phillip . . . he must have real-ized what she'd done . . . he must have . . ." Elisabeth turned away from the girls for the first time since they'd entered the room. She put her head in her hands and her shoulders trembled. Tears streamed down Abigail's face, too.

"He killed her, didn't he?" Abigail choked out. "Master Miles killed my mother."

Lucy's mother pulled out a handkerchief and wiped her eyes. She straightened, ready to answer. She opened her mouth to speak. But before she could get the words out, the stateroom door opened, and Phillip Miles appeared in the doorway.

36

ISABELLA

11:30 p.m. Sunday, April 14, 1912

Isabella knew at once that Phillip Miles was drunk. She could smell the whiskey and see his eyes roaming the room, unfocused. They halted on her and narrowed to dark slits.

"What is she doing here?" he demanded.

Isabella blanched, but her mother appeared quite unfazed.

"What's the matter, Phillip?" she asked derisively. "Don't you recognize our younger daughter?"

Phillip Miles stood stock-still for several seconds, as if the words his wife had spoken couldn't penetrate his brain. His face turned dark red. A vein on his neck pulsed. And then, as if he didn't recall what had transpired only a moment before, he laughed. Isabella fleetingly wondered if he was beyond drunk—if perhaps he had lost his mind.

"Have you forgotten to take your tonic again, my dear?" he said with false kindness. "You poor, feeble thing. Your delusions are getting the best of you. Letting thieves into our staterooms and entertaining their falsehoods! Why, I've already met this lying urchin on deck, but I wasn't fooled by her play for my money, not for a single moment!"

Isabella winced, but Lucy was up and moving toward her father. "She is not deluded, Father," her older sister stated boldly. "In fact, I'm quite sure it is *you* who is delusional."

Phillip raised a hand to strike Lucy, but Elisabeth jumped to her feet, shoving her chair back with so much force it seemed as if the entire ship shuddered. She strode toward him.

"Don't you touch her," she enunciated, her face now inches from his.

Phillip Miles laughed again. "And who is going to stop me?"

Without even thinking about it, Isabella found herself stepping forward to stand by her mother's side. Within seconds Lucy and Abby were there as well, creating a wall of strength that forced Phillip Miles to take a step back. He stumbled into a chair and nearly fell, then caught himself, leaning heavily on the chair for support.

"I won't stand for this!" he bellowed angrily. But Isabella heard the waver in his voice, the uncertainty. She heard the fear.

"No, Phillip," Elisabeth corrected him. "It is *we* who will not stand for this. I'm telegraphing my brother immediately. You can expect police to be waiting when we reach New York." She put her arms out and gathered the girls— including Abigail—to her side. Isabella's heart filled with pride as she faced her father. There was no doubt he was a scoundrel, but she was no longer alone. And now she was certain . . . they were stronger.

Her mother straightened, raised her chin, and spoke firmly. "Phillip Miles, your treachery will not divide this family a moment longer."

37

ABBY

12:10 a.m. Monday, April 15, 1912

Abby stood close to Lucy, the word *family* echoing in her ears and making her heart ache. She had spent much of the last day with the sisters, marveling at how alike they were, how much they loved each other despite the fact they'd only just met. And then watching Elisabeth respond to the news with such an open, honest heart made her realize why her mother respected Mistress Miles as she did, and also why she despised her husband.

Now she knew that it was her mother who had brought these women back together. It was this fact that filled her with equal parts pride and heartbreak, because it had cost her mother her life. Maggie O'Rourke was dead. Abby's family had been destroyed by the man standing not five feet from her.

"You killed her!" Abby suddenly screamed, lunging at him. "You killed my mother because she knew what you had done!"

Master Miles's scowl hardened into a sneer and he pushed Abby away, sending her into another chair. "Your mother was a meddling—"

The insult was not out of his mouth when the stateroom door burst open and Felix appeared. "Abby! Abby! We've hit an iceberg!" the boy shouted.

Abby blanched at the sight of her little brother. He wasn't supposed to be here. He was putting himself in terrible danger! "Felix!" she cried, alarmed.

Felix looked from Master Miles to his sister to the rest of the people in the room, and back to Abby. He appeared to realize, quite suddenly, that barging into the stateroom to warn his sister wasn't a wise choice. Still, he plowed ahead. "Abby, we have to get on a lifeboat!"

Abby's eyes widened. "Felix, what are you talking about?" She moved toward her brother, trying to get between him and Master Miles, though she knew the damage had been done.

"Listen to me, Abby," Felix insisted. "They're loading women and children. We need to get to the lifeboats. The ship is sinking."

An iceberg? Lifeboats? It sounded impossible. And Felix *did* have an active imagination.

"Where did you hear this?" she asked. If he'd been belowdecks with the crew he might have overheard a tall tale . . .

Master Miles shoved his way past Abby, weaving only slightly, and glared down at Felix. "What are *you* doing here?" he bellowed, his moustache trembling. "You're supposed to be in a London workhouse! You don't belong on this ship!"

"I came on board with my sister, of course!" Felix boasted, planting his small fists on his hips. "And I've been all over this ship, including the boilers! I was just up on the bridge!"

Enraged, Master Miles turned and slapped Abby hard across the face. "How dare you disobey me!"

Abby gasped and raised her hand to her face while the painful sting spread across her cheek.

"Phillip, no!" Elisabeth cried, coming toward him. But Felix was closer.

"Don't you touch my sister!" he shouted, kicking Miles's shins and biting his arm.

"You vulgar little animal!" Miles bellowed as he swooped down to grab Felix. The boy wriggled away, but Miles came after him again and caught him by the arm. Yanking him upward, he threw him over his shoulder and half stumbled, half ran out of the room.

"Felix!" Abby raced after them but the door slammed closed in her face before she could get to it. An instant later she heard a decisive click.

"Felix!" Abby cried again, yanking at the handle. It didn't move.

They were locked in.

38

LUCY

12:25 a.m. Monday, April 15, 1912

"We're locked in!" Abby shouted from the door, her face stricken. Lucy felt her breath catch in her throat. The horrible scene she had just witnessed was awful enough, but another worry was growing in her unsettled mind. Was Felix telling the truth? Had they actually struck an iceberg?

"There must be another key," Elisabeth said, calmly crossing the room to search through the desk drawers. Lucy followed, and together they began to hunt through drawers and cabinets.

The boy was probably asleep and had a nightmare about an iceberg, Lucy found herself rationalizing as she shifted through papers. Yes, that was it. Abigail always said he had an active imagination. He had woken from a nightmare and come searching for his sister for comfort. She so wanted to believe that this was precisely what had happened, but over the room's commotion she sensed an odd quiet—one she hadn't felt since they'd left Queenstown three days prior.

The ship's engines had stopped.

What would cause them to shut down the engines in the middle of the Atlantic Ocean? she wondered. She considered asking the question aloud, but what good would it do? All they needed to do now was figure out how to get out of the stateroom. The *Titanic* was unsinkable. Everyone said so.

"Do you hear that?" Isabella asked, pressing an ear to the door. "There are people in the corridor." She turned to face the paneled wood and pounded with her fists. "Hello! Hello! We're locked in! We need to get out!" But the voices receded as the people in the passage moved away. "Help!" she cried again.

Abigail looked at Lucy with tears in her eyes. "What will he do to Felix?" she asked plaintively. "He's all I have left in the world."

Lucy had no answer.

Elisabeth left the drawer she was searching, walked to the maid, and wrapped her into a hug. "We will get out and we will get to him," she vowed.

Abigail nodded while Elisabeth wiped her cheeks.

"Now where else might a key be?" Lucy asked, hoping a little distraction would help. "Where shall we look?"

"I'll check the drawers in Phillip's bedroom," Elisabeth replied. "And, Abigail?"

Abby turned, and Lucy's mother lifted her chin and looked her square in the face. "There's something I need you to remember."

"Yes?" Abigail replied.

Lucy watched her mother lean in and give Abigail a kiss on the forehead, watched Abigail squeeze her eyes closed with emotion. "You also have us."

39

ISABELLA

12:35 a.m. Monday, April 15, 1912

Isabella climbed onto the sofa to look out the small window. The door was locked, but they might be able to find another way out. She blinked, surprised to see so many people on deck so late at night—the clock on the mantel said it was well after midnight. Perhaps Felix's story about hitting the iceberg was true!

"What do you see?" Lucy asked from the desk.

"An awful lot of people," Isabella replied. She pressed her face against the glass to widen her view and spotted uniformed crewmembers uncovering lifeboats, preparing to swing them over the side of the ship for lowering.

"And crewmembers preparing lifeboats," she added with alarm.

Everyone in the room stopped what they were doing and turned to her.

"So it's true!" Abby cried, a fresh wash of tears springing to her eyes.

"Girls, listen to me." Elisabeth's voice was steady and firm. "We must stay calm. I am sure the evacuation is a precaution, but you heard what Felix said—they are loading women and children first. That is us. We will find a way out of here, find Felix, and get to a boat. We cannot panic."

Isabella reached up to unlatch the window . . . perhaps she could open it and they could climb out onto the deck. But the metal latch had frozen closed.

"Let's bash it in," Lucy suggested, her face determined. She picked up a brass lamp from the writing desk. "This looks heavy enough."

Isabella moved aside while Lucy climbed onto the couch and raised the lamp over her head. She was about to hurl the lamp into the leaded glass, when there came a sharp knock on the door.

40

ABBY

12:45 a.m. Monday, April 15, 1912

Abby heard the knock and rushed to the door. "Hello! We're trapped in here!"

The lock clicked, and a moment later the door opened. Jasper stood in the doorway wearing a white life belt and an extremely worried expression.

"Oh, thank goodness you're all here," he said. Abby was thanking each of her lucky stars. She threw her arms around Jasper without thinking, then pulled back quickly.

"I'm so glad to see you!" she said breathlessly.

"Is Felix with you?" Jasper asked.

"No!" she cried in anguish. "Master Miles has him."

"Master Miles?" he echoed. Jasper's face shifted into an

expression Abby had never seen before—an intense combination of fear and worry. Behind him, the corridor was fill-
ing with passengers. Some of them wore heavy coats; others
wore only their nightclothes. Most had vest-like life belts
over their clothing.

"Girls, we must dress warmly." Elisabeth walked to the
wardrobe and began to pull out the heaviest overcoats,
distributing the garments.

"Put these on over your coats." Jasper located the life
belts in the wardrobe and passed them around.

"Tell me the truth," Elisabeth said softly, looking Jasper
in the eye. "Is the *Titanic* sinking?"

Jasper nodded, his face grim.

"But the *Titanic* is unsinkable!" Lucy declared. "We've
heard it said over and over!"

"She's made of steel and is taking on water," Jasper
replied gravely. "And there's nothing we can do to stop it."

Elisabeth put a hand on her daughter's arm reassuringly.
"I'm sure there are other boats in the area that will come to
our aid."

Abby turned to Jasper, whose face was a mask. "Let's
hope so," he replied, and together they hurried out of the
stateroom.

41

LUCY

12:55 a.m. Monday, April 15, 1912

Isabella handed Lucy her green coat as they were pushed into the corridor. It was crowded now, and they were mashed against the passengers making their way to the boat deck.

"No, you take it!" Lucy told her little sister. "I have the blue one." She tried to slip an arm into the coat but a young boy careened into her, putting her off-balance. She righted herself and paused to get the coat and her life belt on, only to find herself well behind the others. She could just make out Abby up ahead, craning her neck to try to spot Felix and her awful father.

Her awful, awful father. Just thinking about him made Lucy's entire body cringe. She pushed him out of her thoughts and, using her small stature to sneak through the crowd, caught up to the group and took her mother's arm.

"Thank goodness," her mother said, clearly relieved. "We need to stick tightly together." Lucy smiled and reached for her sister's hand. Her father might be the most despicable man on the ship, but her mother was more wonderful than ever. And, perhaps more importantly, stronger than ever.

At the end of the corridor a small mob of people was waiting to get out onto the deck. As they drew closer Lucy understood why . . . the boat deck was swarming with passengers. The temperature had dropped from chill to freezing, and their breath hung in clouds about their faces. Shivering, Lucy buttoned the top button of her coat.

Isabella trembled beside her and tightened her grip on Lucy's hand.

"Stay close," Jasper said over the shouts of the crowd. He was two heads up in the throng and Abby was with him. "And follow me."

Lucy could hear the band playing, but could not tell exactly where the music was coming from. Someone fired a rocket into the air, momentarily lighting up the night sky and the panicked faces of the passengers.

Isabella gazed up at the last lights from the rocket curiously. "I've never seen fireworks before," she said. "They're so beautiful."

It was true. The sky was clear and the stars shone sharply, like ice crystals suspended in the inky cobalt sky. They seemed to be winking in the cold air.

"They're signaling other ships," Lucy explained, squeezing her little sister's hand. What a remarkable thing to see beauty at a time like this! "But yes, they are beautiful," she agreed. She turned her gaze back to the mass of people ahead of them, searching the backs of the heads looking for Abby and Jasper. The ship was starting to tilt to starboard, and she had to be careful about where she put her feet on the frozen deck so she didn't slip.

"Where is Abigail?" she called to her mother, just as a group of anxious men was pushed backward and right into them.

"Women and children only!" a crewmember shouted at them. "No men!"

A moment later, someone shoved the three women forward.

"We are loading women and children! Step forward please!" the crewmember shouted. But Lucy couldn't move. Something inside was holding her back.

"Mother," she said. "We need to—"

She was interrupted by a surge in the mass of people behind her, and felt herself being shoved forward by the force of the mob. A moment later she lost hold of Isabella's hand.

42

ISABELLA

1:05 a.m. Monday, April 15, 1912

Isabella felt her hand slip from Lucy's grasp and her body being pulled away from the lifeboats. Which, oddly, did not fill her with panic. She could see Abby and Jasper off to one side, and knew they weren't going to board. Having finally found her own sister, Isabella understood that nothing would keep Abby from trying to find and save her little brother if it were humanly possible. And she suddenly knew it was possible!

"I know where Felix is!" Isabella shouted in Lucy's direction, though it wasn't at all clear whether Lucy could hear her over all the shouts and booms and hissing steam. "Get . . . Mother . . . onto . . . a . . . lifeboat," she yelled as loudly as she could. It felt so strange to call Elisabeth Miles *Mother*, and stranger still to leave her mother and sister when they had only just been reunited. But Isabella knew she could help Abby find—and possibly save—Felix.

She knew what it was to be alone. To be so lonely your heart felt as if it were going to crack open in your chest. If there was any way she could save Abby from that fate, she absolutely would.

"Abby, wait!" she shouted in the other direction. Ducking elbows, Isabella forced her way through the crowd. She lost her footing when another rocket went off and distracted her, but quickly scrambled back to her feet.

Breathless, Isabella caught up to Abby and grabbed her elbow, startling her. "This way!" she cried.

"Isabella!" Abby shouted over the din. "I thought you were on a lifeboat!"

Isabella shook her head. "I think I know where Phillip Miles is," she said. "This way—hurry!"

43

LUCY

1:10 a.m. Monday, April 15, 1912

Lucy could still feel the warmth of her sister's hand when she was pushed forward yet again and lost sight of Isabella completely. The *Titanic* was not only listing starboard now, the bow was also angling down, pointing toward the depths into which it was clearly headed. Anyone who thought the ship unsinkable was being proven wrong with each passing minute. Lucy felt her mother slip and pulled on her arm to keep her from falling.

"Lean on me," Lucy said as she struggled to keep herself upright.

"We can lean on each other," her mother replied.

"Women and children!" a crewman loading lifeboats

continued to shout. He assisted a woman and her two sons into the center of a lifeboat while two more crewmen waited and held tightly to the ropes that were attached to massive pulleys, ready to lower the boat into the dark water below.

"I don't want to board," Lucy said, looking over her shoulder. Not that she actually expected to see anything behind her other than a mob of strangers. The boat deck was becoming more and more chaotic by the second as more and more passengers understood that this was not a drill . . . or a precaution. The *Titanic* would not be afloat much longer.

"I don't want to go without them, either," her mother said. "We just found our Isabella!" It was hard for Lucy to see the anguish on her mother's face—like physical pain. They were shoved roughly forward again.

"Get on the boat or get out of the way!" said a woman, clearly wearing every jewel she owned, and carrying a small dog as she elbowed past them.

Lucy's mother stepped back, away from the lifeboat. The anguish on her face disappeared, and her expression became resolute as she turned to Lucy. "We go together or not at all," she said. But before they could move farther away, the crewman loading the boat grabbed Lucy's arm.

"Time to board, miss," he said. "It's now or never." Lucy felt herself being lifted off her feet as a gentleman on her other side picked her up at the elbow. The two men lowered her into a lifeboat that was ringed with seats and fitted out with oars.

"Mother!" she shouted in alarm.

"I'm here, Lucy," Elisabeth replied as she, too, was lifted into the boat. "I'm right here." They had no choice now, and there was no turning back. Lucy and her mother found seats and did not speak for several long moments, both of them searching the mobbed boat deck for familiar faces. "I'm sure Isabella and the others will be on the next one."

Lucy suspected that her mother didn't believe that any more than she did, but she had to have faith that if Isabella and Abby and Felix were not on the next lifeboat, they would be on the one after that. She simply had to hold out hope; it was all she could do . . .

"We just found her," Elisabeth whispered. "We will get her back."

Lucy squeezed her mother's hand, swallowing the lump in her throat. The stars overhead blurred, and a moment later the crewman shouted and the lifeboat began to jerk down toward the dark and icy Atlantic.

44

ABBY

1:20 a.m. Monday, April 15, 1912

"Are you sure you know where he is?" Abby asked. She could feel hope rising in her chest as Isabella led her and Jasper down the aft Grand Staircase. They pushed past the rest of the passengers, all of whom were making their way *up*.

We're going the wrong way, she thought, but quickly banished the idea. *You can't think like that*, she scolded herself. Besides, finding Felix was all that mattered.

Abby was extremely grateful to Isabella—a girl she had as recently as yesterday called a coat thief—for her help. She could have easily climbed aboard a lifeboat with her new-found sister and mother and rowed out to safety. There was no reason she should care about a maid and her stowaway brother. But she did.

As they stepped off the bottom stair, Abby's stomach bobbed. The stern of the boat was beginning to rise and the angle made it hard to navigate the stairs.

"The bow is sinking," Jasper said gravely. "Where are we headed?"

"The first-class smoking room," Isabella replied. They pushed through a spinning door, ignoring the "no women allowed" rule, and stepped inside the smoking lounge. Even in her panic, Abby noticed how beautiful the room was with its carved mahogany paneling inlaid with mother-of-pearl. The stained-glass windows were so tall they reached above the floor of the boat deck. But not an inch of the opulent fittings, nor the rigid class rules, would help keep the *Titanic* afloat.

"Where is he?" Abby asked, wringing her hands. "I don't see him!" The room was nearly empty, save a few men huddled together. Abby wondered why they weren't up on deck getting into boats. Surely the women and children would soon be loaded and they would begin loading the men . . .

"Abby!" a voice called.

"Felix!" Abby rushed to an alcove, where Felix was tied

to a chair with a curtain cord. She was so happy to see her brother she didn't see Phillip Miles leaning on a nearby mantle. He'd secured the boy so he could help himself to some whiskey.

It was no surprise that Phillip Miles would depend on liquid courage—it was the reason Isabella had known where he would be.

"Not so fast," Miles slurred, lurching in their direction. Jasper calmly stepped between them and knocked the bottle out of Miles's hand. But before he could move away, Miles backhanded him. Fueled by anger and assisted by the listing ship, the force of his slap sent Jasper sliding across the room. He crashed into a chair and lay on the floor, moaning slightly.

"Jasper!" Abby and Isabella called out in unison. Isabella rushed to his side. Part of Abby wanted to rush to him, too, but she needed to free Felix. Now.

"Fools. You should save yourselves," Miles slurred, half laughing at Isabella and the fallen boy. "You're all children. They would let you board a lifeboat."

Abby focused on untying the knots around Felix's wrists, trying to ignore what the terrible man was saying. The cords were tightly tied, pressing into her brother's skin. Her slender fingers tugged frantically but the knots did not yield. Finally, she managed to loosen an end, but out of the corner of her eye she could see Miles wobbling closer.

"Leave the boy. He's mine!" Miles shouted, and lunged. He reached out and yanked Felix to his side, gripping him so tightly that his knuckles turned white. "You're my ticket onto one of those lifeboats," he said.

"I'm not going anywhere with you!" Felix shouted, trying to punch his captor.

Abby grabbed for her brother, and missed. "No!" She caught Miles's free arm and pulled, pleading with him to release her brother.

Miles tried to shake her off. When that didn't work he kicked her, buckling her leg and sending her careening into Isabella and Jasper. The three of them tumbled into one of the square tables and were pitched to the sloping floor.

"Abby!" Felix tried to wiggle free, but Phillip Miles only tightened his grip. And before anyone could stop him, he raced away, half carrying and half dragging the only family she had in the world.

45

ISABELLA

1:40 a.m. Monday, April 15, 1912

Isabella struggled to find her footing on the slanting floor as she watched Phillip Miles retreat. Abby was back on her feet in an instant, but Jasper had landed badly. He had to use the wall to pull himself up. The table had tumbled onto one of his legs, and Isabella noticed he wasn't bearing weight on it.

"I have to go after them!" Abby cried, though she didn't need to explain. Felix's frantic shouts were already fading.

"Go!" Isabella told her. She offered her shoulder to Jasper and they followed as quickly as they could, limping along and using the walls for support.

By the time they emerged on the boat deck, Abby had disappeared. Jasper scanned the deck, pointing toward the rail, and they made their way through the milling crowd. The hundreds of remaining passengers were stumbling about, stunned or panicked, and many were shrieking. Isabella wanted to push them all out of her way. Her situation was dire! But, she quickly realized as she took in the scene, so was everyone's. She shouldered her way through as best she could, trying not to think about how many people were still aboard and hoping that her mother and sister were not amongst them.

"Almost all the lifeboats are gone!" Jasper said, leaning over the rail to assess the crowd. He squinted toward the back of the boat.

"That's nonsense!" a man behind them shouted. "There have to be more boats. They haven't finished loading the women and children!"

Despite the man's words, Isabella realized that Jasper was speaking the truth. She could only see two boats from where she was standing—one being lowered on ropes, though it was only half-full—and another just being loaded. But how could that be? There were still hundreds upon hundreds of passengers on board!

Surely there were more lifeboats on the other side . . . and in the rear . . .

Besides tilting and sloping, the *Titanic* was riding lower in the water—much lower. The dark ocean felt far too close. Riding a wave of panic, the crowd surged toward the last visible boat. Isabella was pushed against the rail and saw a man leap for the lifeboat being lowered down the side. Screams and shouts of fear and protest . . . and then horror filled the air as the desperate man missed and plummeted into the Atlantic.

"Please remain calm," one of the crewmen shouted. His voice was drowned out by the panicked cries of the people around them.

Isabella scanned every face she could, looking for Abby, Felix, Miles . . .

Some men, realizing there would be nothing left for them to board, were lashing together deck chairs in an attempt to make a raft. Others were simply flinging the chairs over the rails in the hopes they would offer someone something to cling to.

"Abby!" Jasper called again and again. "Abby!"

Isabella continued to search each face, looking for one that was familiar, but saw only despair, despondency, and hysteria. Every face told a story. It was unbearable, and yet she could not stop searching. She looked into the eyes of the crewman loading the boat. He'd lost control of the situation and his expression was perhaps hardest to bear. It was his job to help these people . . . and he could not.

Suddenly gunshots rang out so close that Isabella was deafened. For a moment the world lost all sound. Then over the ringing that replaced the silence she once again heard Jasper's desperate cries. "Abby! Felix!"

46

ABBY

1:45 a.m. Monday, April 15, 1912

"Let me through! I have a child!"

Abby froze. Phillip Miles was directly behind her, trying to board a lifeboat with her brother! She would recognize his horrible voice anywhere. In her panic and the chaos on the crowded boat deck she'd gone right past them. She turned quickly, colliding with a pair of people clinging to each other beside the boat rail.

"I'm sorry!" she mumbled as she skirted around them.

The woman was hysterical. "I won't go without you," she wailed.

And I won't go without my brother, Abby thought.

She thrust herself forward and spotted Miles's unmistakable moustache.

"I must go with my son. I am the only family he has," Miles insisted, trying to push past the crewman blocking him.

If she hadn't been so petrified, Abby might have laughed at the absurdity of his words. Phillip Miles had Felix in his arms and her brother was hitting and kicking him in a blind fury. Miles was holding him tight and flinching as Felix pummeled his face, screaming, "You are *not* my father. You are *not*!"

"Women and children only!" the crewman insisted. "I can only take the boy!" He reached his arms out for Felix, but Miles jerked Felix backward to keep him out of the crewman's reach.

"Felix!" Abby shouted into the din. Miraculously her brother heard her voice. They locked eyes as Miles was forced back by the coursing crowd.

"Load the boy!" someone shouted. "This may be his last chance!"

The rest of the boats on the second class promenade had already been lowered. People were shouting that there were no more boats left on the starboard side.

Several people began to grab for Felix. Miles stumbled, fell, and sprawled on the deck. The moment Miles loosened his grip, Felix scrambled away and was instantly swooped up by another man. Abby felt a wave of panic as she raised her head to look at the tall man standing before her.

"Mr. Greer!" The man looked as surprised to see Abby as she was to see him.

"Felix!" Abby cried.

"This is your brother?" Mr. Greer asked. He thrust Felix into Abby's arms before she could answer. "Get on a boat, both of you," he said. "Quickly."

"Stop them!" Phillip Miles struggled to his feet, shouting.

"Don't worry about him," Mr. Greer said. "That sorry excuse for a man has traded one terrible fate for another. Now go."

"Stop them!" Phillip Miles shouted again. Abby couldn't speak, but nodded her thanks to Mr. Greer and fled, not waiting to see if anyone else was paying attention to her master's demands. She certainly wasn't. And she never would again.

Leading Felix by the hand, she hurried up the inclined deck toward the stern of the ship. She looked back once to see if anyone was following. Most people paid them no attention. But Miles, alone, was clambering maniacally up the deck after them.

47

ABBY

1:55 a.m. Monday, April 15, 1912

The boat deck was in utter chaos. The lights of the *Titanic* blazed brightly, almost mocking the desperate scene. The ship was doomed, and yet with her brother's hand clasped safely in hers, Abby was determined to survive.

"There you are!" Abby cried at the sight of Jasper and Isabella making their way across the crowded boat deck. She was so overcome with relief her knees felt weak. Or was that the listing of the ship?

"There are boats back here." Jasper turned in the direction Abby had come.

"No. This way." She didn't have time to explain that Miles was coming and the last boat behind them was about to be lowered. She prayed there was room in the boats at the stern.

Jasper did not question. He leaned forward and tried to propel them up the deck.

"Young women and children here," he called as he cut a limping path through the crowd. On the first-class promenade there was still one boat being loaded. Jasper steered them to the front of the line and let go of Abby's shoulder.

"There. Take them and board," Jasper said softly. Isabella took Felix's hand and stepped forward to be helped onto the boat. Abby did not move. She couldn't. They'd made it, but she only now realized that Jasper did not intend to board with them.

"Now," Jasper said gently. "You must go now."

"You have to come with us!" Abby pleaded.

Jasper leaned in and quickly brushed his lips against hers. They were warm in the freezing night and the little breath Abby had was gone in an instant. "They don't need more crew on this boat, but I'll be on the next one," Jasper whispered.

Abby could not speak. They both knew that the next one was probably already gone. Jasper flashed his crooked smile. "I promise," he said. "I still have to convince you to be my sweetheart, don't I?"

Jasper took Abby's elbow and helped her to the edge of the boat. She felt numb.

"Keep out of mischief," he yelled down to Felix. "At least until I'm there to help you get out of it. Keep each other safe!" he shouted to Isabella.

Abby drew a breath, her mouth opened slightly. There were so many things to say, but she couldn't get a single word out. She stepped onto the boat and sat down beside her brother. The men began letting out the ropes hand over hand. The air was filled with plaintive cries. The boat lurched toward the dark water and her heart lurched with it. Abby looked up at the deck, searching for Jasper. She looked and looked, squinting and hoping to catch a glimpse of him, wishing she had said something . . . anything.

But Jasper was already gone.

48

LUCY

2:10 a.m. Monday, April 15, 1912

Lucy sat frozen. Unable to move or think, and it had little to do with the temperature. She couldn't take her eyes off the hulking ship rising out of the water as they rowed away. The massive propellers at the back of the ship were lifting out of the ocean and streaming water while the bow dove below the surface. The sinking *Titanic* was too big. Too impossible.

"Don't look," her mother said. Elisabeth pulled her daughter's head down to her shoulder as the crewmen on their lifeboat rowed farther from the ship. But Lucy could not see anything else . . . even with her eyes closed.

Opening her eyes, she stared unblinking. The night was clear, the dark water almost glassy. And the *Titanic*, in spite of her alarming angle, was still aglow with electric light. Every lit portal was a stark contrast to the black water.

The freezing temperature made shimmering waves in the air, but Lucy could make out shapes—people or perhaps furniture—sliding down the decks and into the water. She saw others jump and heard screams and moans. And also music. The band that had set up by the Grand Staircase to soothe the passengers was still playing.

The stern continued to rise like a column until it was nearly perpendicular to the water. Lucy grasped her mother's hand tightly.

Please let Isabella and Abby and Felix be safely aboard another lifeboat. Please oh please oh please. She repeated the words over and over in her head while tears began to stream down her cheeks.

With the groan of yielding metal, the enormous forward funnel collapsed and splashed down into the water, instantly sending many passengers who'd fled overboard to an icy, watery grave.

Lucy stared at the horrifying image until it became

unbearable, then buried her head in her mother's lap and covered her ears. Elisabeth stroked her daughter's hair and made soothing noises, but the horrific images still flickered behind Lucy's closed eyes.

The screams and cries for help could not be blocked out.

49

ISABELLA

2:15 a.m. Monday, April 15, 1912

Isabella shivered. Her skirts were wet and so was the bottom of the green coat, but it was the chilling image of the *Titanic* nearly standing on end that was causing her to quake like a leaf. She could scarcely breathe. The freezing air hurt her lungs and stung her eyes. The sound of everything in the ship being thrown against the walls, deck chairs and people being tossed into the freezing sea, was almost as horrifying as the scene before them. And the frantic cries for help coming from the people in the water were indescribably haunting.

Beside her, Abby clung to her little brother. She tried to hide the boy's eyes but he squirmed away to gape at the unbelievable sight. Isabella understood . . . it was impossible to look away.

Isabella held her breath as the lights of the ship blinked once—and were extinguished forever. Then, with the groan of surrendering metal, the mighty *Titanic* split in two. The passengers on the lifeboats watched in horror as the aft of the ship crashed back into the water, sending out waves, while the bow, released, disappeared into the inky deep.

"Oh!" Isabella cried out involuntarily, and covered her mouth with her hands. She could still see people clinging to the rails of the righted stern, which did not remain level for long. Taking on water through the sheered-off end, it quickly tilted upright once more and sliced into the depths.

The noise of escaping air and yielding metal faded quickly, amplifying the moans and cries of the people in the water. Where once there had been a massive ship, now there was nothing but ice and debris and people struggling to cling to anything that remained afloat.

Isabella swallowed the sob rising in her throat. The two men handling the oars on their lifeboat were still rowing away even though the danger of being pulled under with the ship had passed.

"We should go back," Isabella implored the young man

closest to her. "There are people alive in the water!" There was room in their boat—nearly twenty seats.

"We'll be swamped," the crewman replied tersely. "We need to save ourselves."

"We can't leave them to drown!" Abby argued.

"Please!" Isabella stood up and grasped the sleeve of a crewman but he brushed her off brusquely. The lifeboat rocked wildly and nearly tossed her out.

"Sit down before you kill us all!" someone else yelled.

Abby grasped Isabella's arm and pulled her down. Isabella sat, stunned. She knew Abby was as anxious to go back for survivors as she was—one in particular. She'd seen the kind steward steal a kiss as he helped Abby board. She prayed it was not a final kiss good-bye.

Isabella found Abby's hand in the darkness and held it tightly. She accepted a flask being passed around to warm them, but the burning liquid did little to ease the bitter cold.

Isabella didn't have any tears left to shed, but though her eyes remained dry, inside she wailed for herself, for the people in the water, for the people who had gone down with the ship.

She tried not to notice as the screams and moans of the people in the water grew more faint. She tried not to notice when they stopped completely and the only noises left were the soft sounds of water lapping against the lifeboats and the whimpers of the people inside them.

It was a welcome relief when another lifeboat approached—though the passengers huddled within it looked like Isabella felt: half-dead with shock and cold. Soon another boat joined, then another, and several brave members of the *Titanic* crew instructed everyone to move to spaces on other boats so they could go back with an empty boat to search for survivors.

Survivors. Isabella shut her eyes briefly and prayed they would find people alive, though deep down she knew it was futile. The water was like ice . . . nobody could have survived in it for long.

As the lifeboat passengers shifted, Isabella searched the haunted faces of the people who'd been evacuated on other boats. Disappointment bubbled up as she stared at each stranger—none of them Lucy or Elisabeth Miles. None of them Jasper. On the heels of disappointment came a wicked thought, for there was one member of the Miles family Isabella hoped never to lay eyes on again.

She prayed that Phillip Miles was dead.

50

ABBY

5:30 a.m. Monday, April 15, 1912

Abby slumped over her sleeping brother. She was pleased he was asleep, though she could tell from his twitching body he was already having nightmares about this awful ordeal . . . and it was not yet over. Felix had nodded off soon after they'd spotted the flares—a signal sent from another boat to let them know they were coming to help—and he'd slept on as the stars faded and the ship, the *Carpathia*, came into view.

Abby could not feel her hands or feet—they were numb with cold. Her heart, too, felt frozen. She tried not to look at the water in the brightening day. She tried not to see the hundreds of floating bodies amongst the ice and wreckage when they pulled alongside the *Carpathia*. She glanced at Isabella next to her, but the other girl sat silent and listless as they waited to be taken aboard.

"You there. You're next. Send up the boy."

Abby was jostled and pulled to her feet along with her brother. Felix stood up groggily and was helped toward a cargo net hanging down from the deck of the *Carpathia*.

"Climb on up, boy," the crewman said. Felix looked back.

"Go on," Abby encouraged her brother. She futilely tried to bring feeling back into her hands by pounding them on her thighs, but could feel nothing and couldn't move her fingers at all. Still, as she watched Felix ascend to safety, her heart lifted a bit.

Though the *Carpathia* was not nearly as large as the *Titanic*, it was a long way up to the deck. When it was Abby's turn her hands still felt like lumps of ice. She set her feet in the ropes, but her fingers could not bend to grasp anything. Her strength had left her and she fell back into the lifeboat. She struggled to her feet, desperate to try again, and felt a hand on her arm.

"Wait a moment," Isabella said, pointing up. A deck chair, secured by ropes, was being lowered down to them. When it reached the lifeboat, Abby was strapped inside and was heaved upward, bumping roughly against the side of the boat.

Felix was waiting when she was lifted over the rails of the *Carpathia*, and the chair was lowered back down to bring up more people. Someone she did not know wrapped a blanket around her shoulders, led her to a chair, and put a mug of something warm in her hands. It took several tries to hold the cup, but the man was patient with her. All she felt was cold. All she felt was numb.

Abby was surrounded by other blanket-wrapped passengers sitting in stunned silence. A few moved about, sobbing in relief or grief while the *Carpathia* crew pulled more survivors from the lifeboats.

Many passengers wandered the decks, calling out the names of their loved ones. Some found one another and clung together, weeping. Abby had to turn away. She wanted to look for Jasper, Miss Lucy, and Mistress Elisabeth, but couldn't. She was afraid she would not find them, and she could not face that. Not now. Not yet.

"Abby! Felix!" A familiar voice startled Abby. She stared blinking, unbelieving, up at Constance. Her roommate looked paler than she'd ever seen her. She had dark circles beneath her eyes, but . . . "You're alive!" Constance exclaimed, dropping to her knees in front of them.

"We're alive," Abby said, almost as if she were trying to convince herself. She was alive. Felix was alive. Isabella was alive. Constance was alive. But so many were gone. What were the odds that . . .

"Lucy! It's Lucy!" Isabella stood up and moved unsteadily toward a pair of women wrapped in blankets and holding each other up. Beneath the dark wool, Abby saw a flash of blue—Lucy's coat! Isabella embraced the pair and pulled them back to where Abby and Felix were huddled.

Mistress Elisabeth held each of their faces and kissed both of their cheeks. "Children," she sobbed. "Children." She could not say more.

Abby smiled through her tears. She was happy that Lucy and her mistress had survived, but had never felt less like a child in her life.

Exhausted and overwrought, she staggered away from the reunion to stand next to Constance, who was shockingly silent, and gaze over the ship's rail as people were pulled from the last two lifeboats. She could feel pain as the feeling in her frozen limbs returned—pain from the terrible night—proof she was alive. But still, none of it seemed real.

She and her brother had survived. But from the look of it more than half of the passengers aboard the *Titanic* were gone . . . forever. Most of them men. What were the chances that—

"Say, isn't that your steward?" Constance asked.

Abby blinked unbelievingly. Could it be possible? "Jasper!" she called, her voice a breathless rasp. She watched him being lifted over the ship rail and set down on deck and tried again, as loudly as she could. "Jasper!" The name came out louder, and she pushed her way toward him.

Jasper looked up. He could barely stand on his own, but when he saw Abby his eyes brightened and one corner of his mouth rose . . . the beginning of a crooked smile.

51

LUCY

9:10 p.m. Thursday, April 18, 1912

Lucy gazed over the railing at the lights of New York City as the *Carpathia* made its way into the harbor. The city lights looked like a mirage, but were nonetheless proof that the long week was over, that they had reached their destination. It had been a strange nine days. The 705 survivors, fewer than one-third of the people who had set out on the *Titanic*, filled the smaller rescue boat to bursting and forced everyone to share food and quarters.

Isabella, Abby, Felix, Lucy, and her mother all shared one small room that had graciously been given up by the *Carpathia*'s crew. The crowded accommodations, though a stark contrast to the lavish *Titanic*, suited Lucy just fine.

She did not want to be separated from her family, and though she'd only just met Isabella, and Abby was their maid, she felt as though they were *all* family now. *Real* family. They did not talk much in the close quarters, but their proximity, their presence, the fact of them, was an immeasurable comfort.

Abby's sweet crewman, Jasper, did not bunk with them, but was with them for all of their waking hours during the foggy, stormy passage.

It was dark and nearly nine o'clock at night when they drew close to the city. Nevertheless the dock was crowded with people. It wasn't surprising—the *Carpathia* had been hounded for the last several miles by smaller boats carrying newspaper reporters. Everyone was hungry for news of the disaster.

Lucy had overheard that fifteen hundred people were presumed dead. Some of them had been rich and prominent. All of them had families or people somewhere who were anxious about their whereabouts and hoping that the tele-graphed news from the *Carpathia* was not true.

A great sense of mourning hung about Lucy like the oppressive fog that had followed them across the Atlantic. The only person she did not grieve for was her father.

Phillip Miles was among those believed to be dead.

For the first three days, Lucy and Isabella had talked to as many passengers on the *Carpathia* as they could, wanting to confirm this belief. They asked anyone who would listen if they had seen a dark-haired man with a particularly large moustache. Others were doing the same—so many men had gone down with the ship—and no one suspected that the hope of the Miles girls was the opposite of most.

Finally the *Carpathia*'s crew finished making a manifest. When Lucy ran her finger down the long list of everyone aboard and saw that her father's name was not on it, the only thing she felt was relief.

Of course it did not stop her heart from aching for the vast number of people who'd perished in the icy waters, or those they'd left behind. There were orphans on board, and rumors that the majority of the families traveling in steerage hadn't even made it to the boat decks. The migrating families had been told too late that the evacuation was not precautionary. And if they had made it to the deck? What then? Lucy thought of the children she'd seen playing, and their doting parents. Many of the lifeboats were less than half-full—there was plenty of room for more children—but there was no doubt that there had been too few boats. Save a few men who had managed to swim to one of the overturned lifeboats or were plucked from the ocean shortly after the sinking, every unlucky soul who had ended up in the frigid water had died. Every. One.

Lucy thought back to the argument she and her mother and two more women besides had had with others in her lifeboat. They'd begged the crewmen to row back immediately—as soon as the danger of being sucked under with the ship was ended. But they, and others, had refused. She would never know if they could have saved just one more person.

A hand on Lucy's shoulder made her start, but she relaxed when she realized it was her mother's, and touched her cheek to it. Isabella was with her, and Abby, too. Felix held his sister's hand on the other side and Jasper was close behind.

They were all together, but so many others . . .

"I wish we could go back," Lucy said softly, "rewind the clocks and start again."

Elisabeth Miles stood behind her eldest daughter with a hand on each of her shoulders. She leaned forward to speak into her ear. "We need to look forward," she said softly. "We have survived so much darkness." Lucy leaned back into her mother, feeling her warmth. "The past will only drown us."

A shiver ran down Lucy's spine and she stared straight ahead. *Yes*, she thought. The lights of the city and noise of the crowd sparked something inside her. A future was waiting there for her . . . for them. She stood a little taller. Her uncle was somewhere in the crowd. Her future was somewhere in that city. Lucy looked at her friends and family lined up along the rail. She took Isabella's hand and squeezed it tight, sharing a look with her sister.

"Now we can move forward, and begin anew," her mother said, loud enough for all of them to hear. She sounded strong and sure, and somewhere deep down Lucy understood that it was for good reason: She was speaking the truth.

ACKNOWLEDGMENTS

The author would like to thank the myriad of dedicated *Titanic* researchers and aficionados who have created a massive and detailed body of research about this historic and tragic event. Though the depths of available material are easy to get lost in, and *Maiden Voyage* is a work of fiction, it is as accurate as possible.

The passengers and crew came to life in unexpected ways during the research and writing process, and the stories of third-class families traveling to America in search of a better life were particularly haunting. Heartfelt appreciation goes to all of the documentarians for keeping their stories alive.

Special thanks to David Levithan for the opportunity to pen this novel, Erin Black for her painstaking review and for falling for the heroines (and loathing the villain) and wading into the deep, and everyone at Scholastic for helping to ensure *Maiden Voyage* was shipshape and ready to launch. Much gratitude!

Lastly, thank you to Stephen Vaughan and our five charming and unruly children for our amazing adventures in life. Without you this ship would never have left the harbor. May we enjoy calm waters and clear vision as we continue our exciting journey together.

S. J.